RICHARD'S REIGN

BOOK SIX
ENTHRALL SESSIONS
A NOVEL

VANESSA FEWINGS

Richard's Reign

Editor: Deborah Kuhn

Cover Artist: Buoni Amici Press

Book layout by www.ebooklaunch.com

ISBN: 978-0-9965014-9-1

For
Mand

"One must still have chaos in oneself
to be able to give birth to a dancing star."

Friedrich Nietzsche

CHAPTER 1

FREEFALLING.

Adrenaline spiking my veins.

Just how I liked it.

Wind whipping my clothes, this rush of air, the peacefulness of nothing.

Thoughts dissipating.

Gravity owning me as the ground drew near.

Skydiving, the wind blasting my face, my body pummeled, death nipping at my heels and the arrogance of knowing I'd survive.

Those painful thoughts returning and my inability to outrun them, or even outfall them, reminding me I'd messed up *again*.

And lost my lover to another man.

The same arrogance that had led me to pursuits like this. The same trust that made me believe giving my girlfriend to my best friend to train was a great idea. A stellar endeavor that was supposed to turn out a world-class submissive. After all, this brilliant dominant who I'd entrusted her to was renowned for his unique talent that turned our lovers into legends. He was also the same person who'd pulled me back from the brink time and time again, saving me in Dr. Cameron Cole's own indelible way. His psychological craft so effective that those of us who endured his special brand of therapy survived it with a sense of having saved ourselves; a profound statement of his brilliance.

Though genius was not without consequence.

This morning I'd told Mia goodbye.

Left her outside Cameron's Malibu beach house knowing full well he loved her more than me, and he was fatefully waiting inside.

No, it wasn't that he loved her more...he loved her differently. The kind of passion I'd never seen in Cameron before, the kind that made him willing to give her up for me.

Cameron and I shared an endearing "bromance" - a connection as strong as brothers. Cameron had counseled me back from the edge of madness, back when my life was all about my father's betrayal and my fiancée's suicide. I'd been there for Cameron, too, when his life had spiraled after his fiancée Zie had betrayed him and he'd called off their wedding. Together we'd gone on the ultimate bender at Chrysalis which had left subs in our wake, giddy and sated. Cameron, me and Shay - our club's head of security - had drunk and fucked our way into mythic status.

Cameron had always been such a private man. A good man. So, I threw myself onto my sword and gave him what he deserved: The love of his life - the woman who was meant to be mine.

I'd lied to myself that Mia would come round and learn the ways of a high-class submissive and enjoy being subjugated as she bowed down to me as her master. She only responded to Cameron like that. Proof that her soul had bonded with his…that only one man could truly set her free.

I'd had no choice but to shake my bad boy ways and do the right thing for once. Even if it meant my heart was going to be ripped out of my chest. Getting over her seemed impossible.

The strike to my back sent me spinning.

A flash of a face.

Brendon, my skydiving partner, yelling…something about pulling my cord. Something about deploying my emergency line.

He shot up and that white cloud of a parachute billowed behind him, sending him rising.

Yeah, good point.

My flesh crawling as I realized the danger.

Fuck.

Plummeting. Spinning. So close to blacking out.

My hand tugging, slipping off and trying again, my breath stuttering to fill my lungs with the air it forgot it needed. The cord ignoring these frenzied attempts, palms sweaty, fingers numb as they fumbled.

Unable to tell which way was up or down—

Refusing to give up, forming my body into a D-arch to slow my rate.

Fucking death in the mouth as the ground came up fast.

A yank backwards and I flew upwards, my canopy cordial enough to respond to that final frantic tug and blasting open, slowing my descent.

Silence surrounding me.

The patchwork ground now a solid color of dark green and fenced off boundaries becoming smaller.

With legs bent, my feet hit the dirt hard and I tumbled into a sprint until the parachute's drag rescinded. I leaned forward, both palms resting on my knees as I sucked in adrenaline- drenched breaths.

My grin widened.

Standing tall I howled my joy.

CHAPTER 2

I STASHED MY parachute in the back of the van, grabbed my backpack and slung it over my shoulder.

God, now I felt better.

Brendon was busy organizing the equipment in the corner of the vehicle. When he saw me he dropped what he was doing and jumped out the back. He grabbed my arm and guided me around to the front. The other five jumpers didn't need to hear this.

"Did your cord fail?" Brendon whispered.

"Little sticky," I said.

"I packed your chute. It passed."

If I told him the truth he'd be on my case.

"What happened up there?" he said.

"It's fine. I'm fine."

"If your equipment failed I need to know."

"User error."

"You're an experienced skydiver, Richard. What the hell's going on?"

"It won't happen again."

"You scared the shit out of me."

"Me too."

He didn't need to hear I'd loved every second.

"Well, as long as you're okay?"

"I'm fine."

He nodded, looking unconvinced. "Any plans for tonight?"

"Have a couple of invites. Tossing up which one's best. You?"

He glanced at the van. "We're all getting together at Universal City. They hook up the East Coast link on the City Walk so you can watch the ball drop in Times Square."

"Sounds great."

"We're gonna eat dinner up there first if you wanna join us?"

"Thanks, I really appreciate that."

"I'll text you the details."

"Great." I gestured I should go.

Head down, I made my way on over to my open-top Jeep Wrangler.

I jolted to a stop.

A young, petite woman leaned against my jeep door, her arms casually folded across her chest, her deep brown eyes flitting nervously.

"Can I help you?" I asked sternly.

She stepped away, realizing the car was mine. "Mr. Sheppard?"

"I'm afraid you have me confused with someone else," I said, spewing the well-practiced lie.

A life lost to the past when I'd distanced myself from my father's illegal shenanigans, namely convincing strangers to trust him with their investments. An endeavor that had ended up losing millions for the trustees, ruining the Sheppard name, which I no longer went by, and landing my father in a North Carolina jail.

The main reason I was living in the desert known as Los Angeles and not New York, the city of my birth and the place I'd never call home again.

"We spoke on the phone?" she said, making it a question.

Lifting my backpack off my right shoulder, I threw it over the jeep door and onto the passenger seat.

I gave her a sideways glance remembering her name as Sienna. Our conversation flashed back. Something about her boss, Andrea Buckingham, wanting to talk to me. Probably to discuss her bad investments or those made by a member of her family after trusting the one-time king of Wall Street.

Fuck. This hell was destined to follow me forever.

I wondered how they'd found me.

Being summoned by one of American's A-list actresses stirred my intrigue. I'd caught a couple of her movies last year that had been surprisingly good. Andrea had been likened to a modern day Audrey Hepburn, but that fame came with an annoying entourage and the paparazzi tight on her heels.

As a solitary man who hated cliques and cameras we were ill-suited to be friends.

"How did you know I'd be here?" I forced a smile.

She shrugged. "When I called you I was outside your home."

A stab of annoyance that she'd followed me here.

Fuck.

"That was impressive." She pointed to the plane. "You kind of left it late to pull your cord."

"Sure that was me?" I glanced back at the van.

"I think so."

She oozed all those interesting traits of servitude that I admired - soft-spoken, polite, and easy to control with a fresh-faced innocence. From her lack of confidence I could tell she was new to this town, vulnerable. Her jeans and T-shirt were all business and her demeanor was that of a loyal personal assistant.

Her plump, sunburned lips and flushed cheeks revealed she wasn't used to this climate. From the way she avoided making eye contact I knew she'd make a stellar sub, a natural. She swallowed her nervousness.

I'd never go for naive again. A promise I intended to keep.

"I've already told you," I said. "I'm spending New Year's Eve with friends." I cursed myself for breaking her stare though she probably wasn't smart enough to catch my lie.

Cameron was with Mia and they'd soon be huddled in a dark corner at Chrysalis, surrounded by mutual friends and celebrating this lord of the BDSM community claiming his prize.

With no intention of having to endure this spectacle of their happiness and my failure, I was actually going to stay home tonight with Winston, my lovable British bulldog.

I had an NFL special to watch and a fifty-year-old bottle of cognac chilling on ice.

"I know it's last minute," she said. "Ms. Buckingham apologizes for the short notice."

"She's forgiven." I opened the door and climbed in.

Sienna ran around to my side and leaned forward. "Look, most men would give their right arm for a chance like this."

"I'm not most men."

"I respect that, Mr. Sheppard. I didn't mean—"

Hearing that old surname made me cringe. I waved her back from the jeep. "I go by Booth."

"Okay, sorry. Mr. Booth."

I gave her a look that told her it was too late. The damage was done.

Sienna seemed panicked.

I remembered the way she'd fawned over her boss at that charity event I'd attended a few weeks ago. She probably served as a loyal friend too. A hard find in this town.

"Send my thanks." I shoved the key in the ignition. "Perhaps another time."

"I shouldn't be telling you this," Sienna burst out, "but Andrea's going to lose the part if you don't help her."

"Part?"

"She's been cast in a secret project and the director's coming down hard on her because she's having trouble."

"What kind?"

"It's a challenging role and Mubarak—"

"The director?"

"Yes."

I arched a brow, my excitement rising having loved his work since I first saw that Oscar winning masterpiece *Nightingale's Fall*. I'd read in GQ that Jack Mubarak was a temperamental Londoner with a special brand of delivering authenticity and pushing his actors hard. His films went well over budget and stretched the schedule way beyond the norm. Being fired off the set could stain an actor's career.

"What's the film?" I revved the engine.

"It's top secret."

"Not sure how I can help."

"That's what she wants to talk to you about." Sienna pulled out her phone, the ringtone bursting out a rapper singing that the world could go to hell.

It made me smile. "Your boss?"

"Andrea must have changed my ringtone."

Which sounded like something I'd do.

"Say you'll come." She handed me a postcard.

I flipped it over and read an address. "What's her role?" I tossed the card on the seat.

"Don't let it fly out."

"What does Andrea want from me?"

"She'd like to discuss that with you privately."

"How about a clue?"

Sienna glanced around self-consciously.

That break in our conversation was all I needed. My Wrangler spun its wheels and sprayed up dust.

I hit a hundred along the dirt path. I couldn't be bothered to glance in the rear view.

I already had a date.

With that Remy Martin, Louis XIII Black Pearl.

CHAPTER 3

THE PHOTOG LOWERED his camera.

Which was a good thing because he was close to getting punched in the face.

From the way he stared at me warily he knew it too.

This was one guest he wouldn't be capturing arriving at Andrea Buckingham's home tonight. I'd drawn his attention after stepping out of the SUV with its blacked out windows and souped-up wheels. A car Shay had insisted on arranging for me when I told him I wouldn't be going to Chrysalis. No doubt under the strict orders of Cameron who was probably keeping track of my whereabouts.

I'd take an Uber home.

A limo pulled up curbside and the photographer joined his wily paparazzo buddies who were thankfully distracted by the man climbing out the back - a young actor I vaguely recognized.

After giving my name to the bouncer at the door, I was allowed in.

The scent of vanilla air freshener and pot hit my nostrils. A small crowd had gathered at the foot of the steps.

I regretted coming here now. I knew no one and this promised to be the worst New Year's Eve on record. I should have trusted my gut.

I turned to go, ready to face the photographers again as I stepped outside.

"Mr. Booth," a female voice said from behind me.

Sienna signaled from the doorway. "Quickly."

A blinding flash.

Fuck.

Retreating back inside I cursed the decision to leave via the front door. I'd managed to maintain a clandestine life since I'd left New York. Why the hell had I agreed to this?

I'd left Winston at home to sulk after promising it'd just be us two. That bottle of Cognac was calling my name. And I thought waiting to pull my cord too long during my jump this morning had been the crappiest decision of the day.

I wondered which website I'd be featured on by the morning. Blinking against the black spots in my eyes, I took in Sienna's short, white dress. She'd pulled her hair up in ponytail, her make-up barely concealing her sun-kissed cheeks.

"You look pretty," I said sincerely.

She started to say something and faltered, as though surprised.

"Nice house." I tried to lessen the tension.

Her frown deepened as she took in my ripped jeans and black J. Crew sweater. Yes, I had noted the dress code had specified black-tie.

I wasn't in the mood.

"The invitation was very specific." Her gaze swept the foyer, taking in the other guests who'd complied as though my *faux pas* could be undone.

"Let's get this over with, Sienna."

"This way." She headed to the west side of the mansion.

I felt the beady eyes of some of the other guests following us down the hallway. We paused outside a door.

"Please be more tactful with Andrea than you are with me," she whispered.

"How'd you mean?"

"Less…"

"Less?" I assumed she meant asshole-esk.

"Andrea's very sensitive."

"In what way?"

Sienna's eyes narrowed and she faced the door.

Great, a temperamental actress used to getting her own way. I mused this might actually be fun, like a cat playing with a mouse kind of fun.

I glanced at my watch and then glared up at Sienna.

She blushed wildly and knocked.

We stepped into an office.

I'd forgotten how breathtaking she was.

Andrea stood beside the desk with her delicate fingers nervously trailing the edge. She was in her twenties but looked younger. She threw a self-conscious glance over at Sienna. This woman had the kind of beauty reserved for super-models or, as my addled brain caught up with my thoughts, A-list actresses.

I was no stranger to women who topped the beauty charts, having been immersed in the elite world of Chrysalis, but this woman's doe-eyed sweetness, her freckled nose and chiseled cheekbones emanated an unearthly innocence. I eyed her voluptuous frame, all curves in a blue mini-dress, long lean legs and - God, if she wasn't barefoot - having kicked off those strappy heels which lay on the floor to her left.

I wondered if her being barefoot was deliberate - perhaps attempting to make this meeting less formal.

My bad boy demeanor was disarmed all over again. Like it had been that same evening we'd been briefly introduced at the Charity Wells Gala at Shutters in Santa Monica. I'd assumed Andrea had forgotten me seconds after my introduction. She'd been whisked away to meet the other guests and hadn't looked back. My gaze, however, had stayed on her as she'd walked away. Not surprisingly she'd been the main focus of everyone during the evening.

I imagined she saw everyone's reaction to her like this...me needing a moment to remember how to breathe. She was gorgeous on screen, but close up Andrea held a dazzling beauty.

"Thank you, Sienna," she said, her voice sounding husky.

Sienna's gaze landed on me suspiciously.

I shrugged, smiling.

Andrea gave a nod to Sienna that she'd be fine and we watched her leave.

"I apologize for the photographers, Mr. Booth."

"Ms. Buckingham, you might want to get yourself a longer driveway."

"I didn't imagine it would ever be quite like this." She lowered her chin. "Please, call me Andrea."

"Richard."

"This home has sentimental value now, so moving is..."

"Great location." I tucked my hands in my pockets. "You're close to the comedy club. Ever go?"

"Once."

"How was it?"

"I went with girlfriends. It was fun."

I was making her nervous. Yet I was trying not to.

I stepped back.

"Thank you for being here," she said.

"Sure. Sienna mentioned you need my help?"

"I've been informed you run a club in Palos Verdes?"

"I see."

She rested her hand on her chest. "This is a little difficult."

I arched a brow, assuming she meant embarrassing.

"Perhaps you'll sign this first?" She lifted an envelope off the desk and offered it to me. "I hope you don't mind."

I took it from her, peeled it open, and slid out the non-disclosure agreement.

"My attorney reads all documents before I sign them."

"It's to prevent you from selling me out to the press, Richard."

"Never going to happen. Who told you about me?"

She shook her head to let me know she wouldn't say.

"Well," I reasoned, "if they know me they'll also be aware how private I am."

"Shall I give you a few minutes to read it?"

I lowered the envelope to my side. "I'll be in touch."

"You're not staying?"

"I'm assuming you want me to sign this first?"

She blushed, looking uncomfortable.

Sienna had mentioned Andrea was struggling with her current role. It didn't take a genius to work out why she'd summoned me.

"Submissive or dominatrix?" I asked.

Now she looked horrified.

"Your role?" I took a step forward.

"This is a little awkward."

"May I take a wild guess?"

"Sure."

"You don't understand the character's true motivation for their need for BDSM."

"And how would you know that?"

"You invited me here."

"I'm playing this character...Rose. I need to experience her surrender."

"Maybe I could take a look at the script?"

"If you could just sign—"

I moved closer, towering over her now and wondering if she wished she'd kept her shoes on for height. "Are you searching out a dominant to talk with about your role?"

"In a way, yes."

I frowned at her vagueness.

"I'm working with Jack Mubarak." She paused as though waiting to see my impressed reaction. "Only this morning he asked me to leave the set and not come back until I learned how to enter subspace." Her lips quivered. "He's demanding authenticity, only I'm not sure what he's asking of me." She stared at me with her soulful brown eyes.

"I see."

"A friend suggested I talk with you."

"Someone in the community?"

"Yes."

"You're not just looking to talk about it are you?" I said.

"Well, if I find the right person who is willing to show me a few moves."

"A few moves?"

"You know, how to be tied up and stuff and not panic."

"Are you dating anyone?"

"Why?"

"Just wondering if there might be a jealous boyfriend I need to be aware of?"

"I'm taking a break from the dating scene."

"So you're portraying a submissive?"

"Yes."

I beamed at her.

"I researched it online," she said.

"Bad idea."

"I know that now."

"It's about getting in the right headspace." I leaned in closer. "Truly surrendering."

She blushed again. "For the role, yes."

"Andrea," I whispered. "Do you really want my help?"

"Please, I'm not into pain."

"Most people aren't."

"So, just so we're on the same page." She narrowed her gaze. "I'm not going to be giving up any control here."

I pulled back on a smile.

"I'll act as though I have relinquished control."

I paused. "Why did you take this part?"

"I need to stretch myself as an actress. The critics have accused me of being one-tone." She shook her head as though trying to shake off those reviews.

"Your agent persuaded you to take the role?"

"It's Jack Mubarak," she said. "I couldn't pass on such an opportunity. He's giving me until after the New Year to prove I'm really dedicated to the role. I need to pull this off. If I lose this…"

"It's not unusual for an actor to pull out of a role."

"Do you think you can help me or not?"

"Sure you really want this part? How about a nice thriller?" I arched my brows playfully.

"I need this," she said softly.

Standing in here alone with another woman shot a pang of guilt into my gut.

Mia Lauren...her laughter, the way she stomped her feet when frustrated. The way she took care of Winston. Took care of me. She'd told me how much she needed me. Needed this.

The same request that Andrea was asking: Blinding domination.

And I'd refused Mia.

My heart would always ache for the woman who was no longer mine and my thoughts returned to this morning when I'd all but delivered her into the arms of my best friend.

I was in no state to take on a needy woman. Even if she was stunning and her servitude would no doubt morph into an easy obsession.

Just the thought of her entourage made my skin crawl. Still, being this close to her elicited the low thrum of arousal. She was gorgeous and taking her hard and fast on that carved wooden desk would serve to soothe this heartache.

Pulling back on my roguish thoughts, I grabbed hold of reason and ran through the scenario of what was best for Andrea.

"Don't make me beg, Richard."

"You mean now or during a session?"

She grazed her teeth along her lower lip. "You seem easy to talk to."

"You're having trouble surrendering on set?"

"Entering subspace. I just can't get there."

"Mubarak needs to see it in your eyes. The camera captures everything."

"Yes."

"You daydream?"

"Yes."

"It's similar. Quiet your thoughts. It's a form of meditation."

Her eyes filled with frustration.

This wasn't just about a role, there was something else going on with her and I felt my interest pique.

"Being a submissive is about finding your center and letting go. Being in the now. Giving yourself over to your lover. Losing yourself and rediscovering yourself at the same time."

Her nipples hardened and nudged the cups of her dress. "I appreciate the insight."

Andrea was subconsciously reacting to my voice, a good sign she'd be trainable.

I reached up and ran my thumb over her bottom lip and she raised her chin in response.

"You know that moment right before you orgasm?" I whispered. "Seconds before you let go and come."

She blushed wildly. "That's very personal."

"Andrea," I soothed. "You asked me here."

Her eyelids blinked rapidly; that tell-tale blush rising on her neck.

"So let me help you."

"You think you can?"

"Most ardently."

"How?"

"That moment when your body is coaxing you to relax and ride the wave of bliss."

She gave a nod as her shoulders relaxed.

"That's subspace."

She stared at me warily.

"Go with it," I said. "Surrender."

Her breathing now rapid, her tongue flitting out to moisten her dry lips.

"That's it," I coaxed, "feel that curl of pleasure between your thighs."

Her eyelids lowered as she tranced out.

"How does your clit feel?"

Her breath stuttered.

"Let that thrill move to your nipples."

Her lips formed an O, her eyelids heavy, revealing that she was luxuriating in this.

"Is that nice?"

She gave a subtle nod.

I held my breath, allowing her to wallow in these sensations. Waiting, watching, and observing each and every clue to her thoughts. The way her pupils dilated…her closeness to orgasm…

The way she moved into me, crushing her pelvis against mine.

"This…" My hardness pressed against her stomach and she moved her hips, teasing, needful. "Is subspace."

"I like it."

I stepped back from her.

She grabbed the back of the desk, blinking rapidly, narrowing her gaze as she rose out of her trance.

I headed over to the door.

"You've forgotten the contract, Mr. Sheppard, Booth, Richard," she said breathlessly.

That made me smile. "Don't need it."

"But before we continue—"

"Session's over, Ms. Buckingham."

"Why?"

"You entered subspace perfectly. You're all good. Replicate that."

I opened the door and left.

CHAPTER 4

MORE GUESTS SWARMED into the foyer.

Those few modern paintings hurt my eyes with their red and gold modernity of unnatural color mixes and I wondered if that was Andrea's taste. New guests were arriving and I forced a polite smile as I weaved around them. A new challenge awaited me - leaving without having my photo taken *again*.

"Mr. Booth," said a husky, annoyed voice.

I spun round—

And peered down at Andrea Buckingham. "Oh, you again," I said flatly.

She folded her arms across her chest. "Mr. Booth, you might want to try a different way out. Avoid the cameras perhaps?"

"Sounds like a plan."

She led me through the foyer to the left of the stairs and I got to witness firsthand Andrea's enigmatic smile as she strolled past her guests, gesturing she'd be right back, their star-struck smiles trailing behind her and landing on me.

Once through another doorway and up some twisting stairs, I knew we weren't heading outside, and I was intrigued. Within a few seconds we were standing in a screening room. Lush red carpet beneath our feet, a low ceiling, leather cream chairs and a thirty foot screen on the wall at the front.

A rush of blood went to my head as I suppressed a grin, wondering if she had an X-box set up in here.

"You owe me an apology," she blurted out.

Having promised myself a home theatre, I took in some pointers.

"You don't do something like that to a woman and then walk out dramatically," she snapped.

"That's how I always walk."

"Are you really this insensitive?"

"Are you really this much of a princess?"

Her slap stung my cheek.

I blinked at her. "Well, glad we got that out of the way."

She looked horrified. "I'm sorry. I don't know what came over me."

Clenching my jaw, I tried to decide just how much of a bastard I wanted to be.

"You're a flirt, Richard."

I shrugged. "You entered subspace. My work is done."

She folded her arms, lips pursed, eyes narrowed on me.

"Andrea, perhaps some self-exploration would benefit you." As she continued to glare at me, I added, "You're having an issue letting go."

"I can let go."

"Do you believe you deserve pleasure?"

"Yes, if I've earned it."

I took a moment to consider that. "Perhaps you could book a session with a friend of mine. This is his specialty. He has connections to Enthrall and—"

"Dr. Cameron Cole?"

I arched a curious brow.

Andrea knew a lot more then she was letting on.

"Richard, apparently you're a little more…"

"More?"

"Less controversial."

How the hell did she know that about Cam?

I also doubted he'd take her on right now. He was too far gone with his new sub and probably not in the right head space.

It was time to shut this down. "How much time do we have?"

"Two weeks."

"Then you're back on set?"

"Yes."

"Do you feel comfortable with your co-star?"

"Yes, he's actually pretty hot." She blushed. "Though he's probably going to get a new leading lady if I can't pull this off."

"What kind of experience are you looking for?"

"Full emersion."

I pulled back on a grin. That would fucking kill her.

She placed her hands on her hips and something told me I would enjoy punishing the petulance out of her.

"Two weeks?" I said. "I can work with that."

"What do you have in mind?"

"I'll introduce you to BDSM." I lowered my gaze. "Gently."

She pressed her hand against her chest. "I'll be your submissive?"

Her face flushed wildly and she looked adorable, her happiness lighting up the room as though she'd been nominated for an academy award instead of agreeing to be lectured for a couple of weeks by my cock.

"Andrea, you have no idea what this means, do you?"

"Not too much pain though, right?"

I was half believing my own lie this was going to happen. "We'll focus on pleasure."

A wave of guilt washed over me that her happiness was going to be short-lived. I was about to rock her world and not in a good way. "Do you agree to obey every order?"

As expected, her joy muted into uncertainty. She hadn't thought this through, apparently.

I ran with it. "Break one order and our agreement ends. Do you understand?"

She nodded. "Thank you," she said. "Let's go and get a drink to celebrate."

"Andrea," I said firmly. "First you must pass the initiation."

She leaned against the back of one of the leather seats.

"Conduct yourself well during this first test and our agreement stands."

"Test?"

"I'll agree to sign your contract so you can relax and enjoy your first session."

"Now?"

"Yes."

"Are we going to make love?"

"You mean fuck? No, you have to earn that right."

She played with a strand of dark hair, twisting it in her hand. "What do you have in mind?"

"Go get your vibrator and bring it to me."

Her cheeks flushed wildly.

And I readied myself for another slap. "Something wrong, sub?"

"I only have a magic bullet."

The visual was enticing.

She looked uncertain. "What are you going to do with it?"

"Meet me back in your office." I glanced at my watch. "You have five minutes. Remove your panties before you present yourself to me."

"Perhaps I can meet you at Enthrall on Monday?" She looked at the door. "My party's started."

"Perhaps you've failed the initiation."

"Does it have to start like this?"

"Trust is the foundation of a master and submissive relationship." She swallowed hard and broke my gaze.

I felt a dull ache of regret this was over, that I'd never know her.

Andrea turned to face me and moved closer.

I readied for that final slap—

She fell to her knees before me and bowed her head.

CHAPTER 5

MY BASTARD DEMEANOR fell away.

Minutes ago, Andrea had quickly risen and left the room to go and retrieve her toy in a flurry of excitement, her cheeks flushed with girly enthusiasm.

She'd performed some kind of Houdini trick on my emotions. My imagination ran wild with all the fun we'd have.

Her mouth was so damn fuckable.

All roguish thoughts morphed into the urge to do the right thing, to get the hell out of here and not going through with this.

And yet here I was heading back to the study.

Her soft floral perfume lingered in her office - that feminine allure that could render a man useless if he let it.

You're going to leave her a note, I reasoned as I pulled one of her notepads towards me and looked for a pen. I scribbled Scarlet Winter's name and number, thinking this renowned dominatrix was a better fit for Andrea. For God's sake, I'd given my last submissive to my best friend to train, that was how averse I was to taking on the inexperienced.

And look where that got you.

The responsibility of mastering a newbie weighed heavily. Very often as the woman explored her sexuality through BDSM for the first time she'd break down into a quivering mess, her psyche surrendering and her heart rejoicing that freedom on this level was possible.

I'd always avoided this stage, choosing instead to take on a sub after they no longer needed to be guided through scenes.

I didn't do vulnerable.

And even if Andrea could never be considered vulnerable, her motivation for putting herself through this was all wrong. Ambition having gotten a hold of her heart and twisting it, forcing her to compromise. Afterward, when she'd reassessed what she'd done for her career the fallout was going to be epic.

I wanted no part of it.

My note was written quickly; a succinct scribbling of thoughts. A session with a dominatrix was more advisable, I told Andrea, reassuring her that my Senior Mistress at Enthrall would be able to handle this. *Handle her.*

A knock startled me and I raised my head to see Andrea standing in the doorway, holding a small box.

She turned and locked the door.

My brain ran through the same excuses I'd been honest about in her note.

She'd changed into a printed wrap dress and as she came closer she tugged the waistband and it fell to her side, her free hand pulling back the material to reveal she'd already removed her bra and panties. Her body was stunningly curvy; breasts pert, nipples pink and erect, that line of pubic hair so inviting, her breathing rapid as she pushed through her bravery.

"Andrea."

She fell to her knees and peered up at me. "Master." She held the box out.

I took it from her.

"I couldn't sleep last night," she whispered. "Knowing I was going to meet you today."

"Who told you about me?" I assumed it was the same person who'd advised her to bow.

Andrea stared up, her eyes wide, her lips pouty, ready to pleasure.

"Tell me," I said firmly, resting the box on the desk.

She hesitated.

And then it hit me—

A woman of this caliber could only come from one man, Cameron *fucking* Cole. The same man who'd set me up with Mia Lauren in an elaborate scheme to force me out of my depression.

The bastard had done it again.

It made sense now…Sienna knowing where I lived, her following me to the jump, her mentioning her boss's dilemma - all a brilliant ruse. I'd felt sorry for Andrea, even though she was probably already a well-trained submissive. She moved too elegantly, her gaze full of respect, awe even, her feminine guile stealing my thoughts and wrapping them around her little finger.

Fuck all of them.

Hadn't they done enough damage?

Being here was too much of a coincidence. Cameron had manipulated my ego, knowing full well I'd wallow in the idea of a stunning brunette of this caliber needing me. He always went for my kind side, which was evidently my weak side.

"Stand."

She rose to her feet and her gaze flitted to the box and then back to me.

I moved away from the desk and gestured she was to stand there now, my hands wrapping around her waist as I lifted her and sat on her on the edge. Seductively, I eased the material off both her shoulders, peeling it off her and it fell around her down to the desk, leaving her naked.

"Good girl," I said.

Her floral perfume filled my senses, her delicate sex alluring.

"We'll go slowly," I whispered, playing along, observing how easily she slid into the scene.

"Thank you, Richard - I mean, Master."

"Better." I ran my hand over her breasts, circling her nipples, avoiding the need to pinch hard, after all I'd promised no pain. "How often do you use your toy?" I took it out of the box and revved it up. Lifting it to her breast, I rested it on her nipple and pummeled the edge of her areola.

"Not that often." Her jaw slackened.

"Why is that?"

"Don't know," she burst out, her expression one of surprise.

"Show me how you use it," I said. "Down there."

She shook her head.

"Are you disobeying me?"

She took the bullet from me and lowered it between her thighs, her cheeks ablaze as she rested it on her clit. She let out a soft moan of pleasure, thrumming the toy up and along. Her expression changed to wonder and as I witnessed her lips quiver, her throat tighten, her blush reaching her chest.

I squeezed my eyes shut to better think. Her stunning beauty was distracting. She had this mystical look about her. And I could see where the Hepburn comparison came from.

Faking these tell-tale traits hinting at inexperience wasn't possible. Or was it? Had Cameron chosen a renowned actress not because of her appeal but her ability to fool me?

Was Andrea Buckingham my consolation prize for losing Mia?

I eased the toy away from her.

She stared at me wantonly, needful of its return.

"Who told you about me?" I said. "You don't come until you tell me."

"I promised," she said, her finger tracing her clit.

"No clit play." I knocked her hand away. Holding her labia apart, my fingertip accidently grazed that erect nub, causing her head to loll back. "Not until you say his name."

She peered through one eye.

"Speak." Again my fingertip found its way, flicking her clit.

"Oh," she moaned, "yes, please."

"Name," I hissed through clenched teeth.

"Can't."

"Name?"

"Please."

"I'm not backing down, Andrea."

"I'll be in so much trouble."

"Do you trust me?"

"Yes."

"It's yes, Master."

"Yes, Master."

"Andrea."

"You mustn't tell anyone."

"You have my word."

"Ethan," she whispered.

My fingers stilled. "Ethan Neilson?"

"He's my cousin."

Her reluctance to tell me made sense. He was a D.A., and a well-respected man. Cameron had worked a miracle on Ethan with his controversial brand of therapy, healing Ethan's erectile dysfunction after a traumatic event and giving him a sex life again. Ethan had become our biggest supporter and an avid member, offering legal protection whenever needed.

I felt like an idiot.

My thoughts were as addled as my heart. I knew Cameron well enough to know he'd not manipulate Ethan into giving up his cousin to me. Cameron was a rogue, but he wasn't Dr. Evil.

Not spending New Year's with him was another strike of bad luck.

She rested her hand on my arm. "Can we keep going?"

My fingers continued their gentle exploration.

"This is okay," Andrea said, peering down, observing the way I absentmindedly flicked her sex. "I'm actually enjoying it."

I only hoped she didn't relay this scene to Ethan. Didn't tell him I'd taken her like this on the desk all too quickly, not following protocol and easing her into this. As the assistant director I was meant to be a consummate expert on all things BDSM.

There should have been role-playing, spanking, teasing. Clothes weren't meant to come off for a while and yet here was one of the most coveted women in the world and she was naked and between my legs, moaning and writhing in my hands. If this was how she responded to clit play she was going to be a screamer when I fucked her.

If I fucked her.

God, she was beautiful.

I searched her face for doubt, any regret, but all I saw was her impending release.

"Good girls are rewarded," I whispered.

"I'm a good girl."

Cupping her cheeks, I kissed her fiercely, feeling her tongue meet mine, that battle of wills beginning as we fought for control, her mouth widening, lips soft, my thoughts scattering.

"I've dreamt of this moment," she whispered.

She soothed me, unknowing of my damaged heart, trusting me with her affection, her future lain squarely in my hands.

"Why is that?" I whispered.

"Because Ethan told me you know how to touch a woman." Her head fell back. "You do. Oh, it feels amazing—" Her stare locked onto my flicking fingers; her thighs trembled.

I saw the look of wonder on her face.

Refusing to fall with her, to let go, I pulled away, remembering the agenda. Andrea wasn't looking for a lover, she needed a knight in shining armor to show her the way of surrender.

I nudged her back so that she lay flat, her legs parted, her sex wet and inviting.

"Hands above your head," I ordered. "Cross your wrists."

She glanced down and watched me spread her thighs wider on the desk.

"What's the longest orgasm you've ever had?"

"Thirty seconds," she said, "I think."

"We can improve on that."

"Oh my God," she mouthed.

Brushing my hands over her breasts, worshiping as I went, caressing soft skin, I felt her shudder beneath my touch as my hands returned to her sex.

Resting my right fingertip on her clit I made a slow, firm circling motion. With my left hand resting on her pelvic bone, I tugged slightly to raise the tension of my touch, and I watched her expression morph from curiosity to intense pleasure.

Our eyes met and she smiled and then giggled, her head falling back again as she looked even more enamored with me.

I slowed my fingertip even more. "What were you expecting, Andrea?"

"To be honest," she whispered, "I wasn't expecting to like it."

"Being trained as a submissive?"

"Yes, I thought you were going to hurt me."

I arched a brow. "Do as you're told."

"Yes, sir. I've never felt anything like this before—" She slapped her hand over her mouth.

I smirked. "No talking."

She gave a nod, her eyes wide with wonder, her glances toward my hand and back to me endearing. Her arms back above her head, wrists crossed over.

"Close your eyes." Keeping that circular motion going with my fingertip, I reached with my other hand for the bullet and flicked it on, then placed the silver oval at her entrance, nudging it inside.

She arched her back as I slid it all along her vagina until it hit her G-spot.

"Be still," I ordered.

"Can't."

"You can and you will."

Andrea trembled violently, obediently remaining still, her dark locks spilling back, that freckled button nose so endearing, her deep-throated groans resonating.

My cock ached and my balls yearned for release but I forced myself to forget my need and concentrate on hers, my fingers soaking wet from her, her scent sweet and alluring, using all my will not to bury my face in her sex and lap at where my finger masterfully thrummed. Her clit would respond well to my mouth.

If I allowed myself the luxury of ever seeing her again.

On and on and on she writhed, riding out her climax, gasping for air, her face taut with a tension that transmuted into a look of pure bliss.

I revved up the bullet and took her higher.

CHAPTER 6

ANDREA PUSHED HERSELF up and wrapped her arms around my neck, snuggling against me, still trembling from her climax.

I caressed her back, running my hands up and down her spine, reaching for a lock of hair and playing with it. Only now did I realize how much I'd needed this spontaneous affection that had seemed so out of reach for me.

She let out a contented sigh. "That was…"

"You okay?"

"That was incredible." She pulled back and rested her nose against mine.

I grinned. "You need to get out more."

She thumped my arm. "My legs feel like jelly."

"You look beautiful when you come. You look beautiful all the time, actually."

"There's something I've never asked you."

"What?"

"Are you seeing anyone?"

I broke her gaze, not wanting to drag my life into this. Being here with her had actually made me forget it. "Of course not."

Her sweetness had a healing effect, and I felt a wave of guilt for all that had transpired over the last hour. This was merely meant to have served as our first meeting, a discussion on how I might help her, and I'd manipulated her into this. Not that Andrea seemed to mind - and from her level of relaxation I could tell she'd needed this just as much as me.

Her expression changed.

I tipped her chin to question the panic evident on her face.

"You didn't sign it?" she asked.

Following her gaze I peered down at the contract.

She picked it up. "Why didn't you sign this?"

"When you left I…" *Had a change of heart.*

She peeled the note open and read it. "I don't understand."

"When you came back you looked so gorgeous…" I broke off, shrugging.

"You're going to the press, aren't you?" She shoved me back. "You'll sell me out."

"No," I snapped. "Never."

"I don't believe you."

"The last thing I need is publicity." I stepped back, putting distance between us.

She looked around the room, her expression full of fear. "Did you bring a camera? Did you record it?"

"Andrea…"

"What am I going to do?" But she wasn't speaking to me - she was racing headlong into a panic attack.

I stepped forward, grabbing the contract and a pen, and then scooped her up into my arms and carried her across the room toward the corner velvet armchair. I sat with her curled up on my lap and I kissed her aggressively, forcing her surrender.

"Richard?" She looked so shaken.

It made me question what kind of breaches in her privacy she'd endured before.

"Shush." I kissed her forehead. "I'm trying to read." I flicked open the contract.

Andrea nuzzled her head into the crook of my neck, and her breathing softened as she watched me turn the pages.

The agreement seemed reasonable enough.

If I signed this I'd be committed to coaching Andrea during her latest project and promising never to discuss the details with anyone. All that had transpired had firmly inserted me into her life for the next fourteen days.

Maybe, I reasoned, this would be good for me. There were no expectations and though this wouldn't be counted as a rebound it could serve as a reasonable distraction to get my mind off this heartache. The kind of pain that swung back around when I least expected it.

Resting the contract on the arm of the chair, I clicked the pen and signed it. "I have a few rules of my own."

"What are they?"

"You keep your entourage away from me."

"They're my friends."

"There's no compromise on that."

"Sure."

"You sign a submissive agreement."

"Okay."

"Well, that was easy."

"I haven't signed it yet."

"Good point."

She raised her head. "What else?"

"We can never be seen together. I don't want my face in the press."

She gave a nod.

My father's enemies wanted my blood, too. If they knew were they could find me they'd unleash hell.

"If I get caught on camera even once our deal is off," I said.

"We'll always meet in private."

I pulled back a little to better see her. "Don't ever doubt me again."

She snuggled against my chest. "I won't."

Pulling her head close against my chest, I marveled how just this morning my life had fallen apart, and yet within hours I was hugging Hollywood's favorite starlet. I liked the idea that no one would ever know about what was soon to become a brief affair. There was something sacred in that.

Andrea fell asleep in my arms.

Rising with this sleeping beauty in my arms, I carried her over to the couch and lay her there, pulling a throw over her.

She stirred.

"Don't sleep too long," I whispered. "You have guests."

"I won't." She let out a long, contented sigh.

I headed out and made my way along the corridor.

It seemed like a good idea to get a feel for Andrea's place and get to know a little more about her. From the look of the crowd, I could see she was submersed in the business. I sensed some of the suits were managers and agents, and I even recognized some of the faces. Had I been in the mood, this might actually have been fun.

A waiter offered me a Miller Lite and I took it, the first sip cold and refreshing. Navigating through the crowd, I arched a brow at the beautiful people, all seemingly privileged, all of them buzzing off the excitement of being here - some of them possibly high.

There were a few throngs of people mingling in the courtyard that led out to a large garden. A fountain changed colors, its light reflecting off the central pool.

I carried my beer out, needing to clear my thoughts and attempt to put into perspective what I'd just committed to.

A woman dived into the pool as I passed her. I dodged the splash as it sprayed up close to my pant leg. A young man stripped down to his underpants and jumped right in behind her. Their playful screams grated on my nerves.

I paused mid-sip. "You've got to be kidding me!"

Cameron turned to look at me.

He stood at the end of the garden beside Mia, and unlike me they'd honored the dress code. Cameron's tuxedo was tailored to perfection and Mia's evening dress followed her curves, the same ones I'd been running my hands over just this morning.

Right before I'd fallen on my sword and given her up.

Cameron beamed back. "Happy New Year to you, too, Richard."

"Thought you'd be at Chrysalis?" I said.

"We chose this instead."

"You know Andrea Buckingham?"

He grinned devilishly.

I rolled my eyes. "When you asked me what I was doing tonight I didn't think you'd gate crash."

"Booth, we haven't spent a New Year's Eve apart in years. It didn't feel right."

I gave his back a pat. "It didn't."

Relief flooded in that he was here and I wasn't going be alone tonight.

My gaze fell on Mia. "Pretty dress." God, her feet looked incredible in those strappy heels.

Just this morning, I'd kissed each pink toe and then fucked her half to death. Had I known it was going to be the last time, I'd have made it more memorable.

It was hard to think straight with her in front of me - she looked so goddamned pretty, so ethereal, all golden locks and innocence.

"Thank you, Richard," she whispered.

Seeing them together like this was going to fucking kill me.

Perhaps they were here to reverse the curse, and Cameron was here to admit his mistake and give her back.

That affectionate swapping of stares between them put an axe squarely in the middle of that fantasy. They were in love and I couldn't ever remember seeing Cameron so ridiculously thrown by a woman before.

"I'll get us some *hors d'oeuvres*." Mia removed Cameron's jacket and handed it over to him.

"It's good to see you, Mia," I said, trying to reassure her.

She stepped forward and wrapped her arms around me. Closing my eyes, I went with this moment. Her soft perfume wafted around me - something expensive that Cameron had bought for her probably - her softness a feminine quality I couldn't live without.

When I opened my eyes again, her gaze was on Cameron.

I clenched my jaw and swallowed my pride. "Mia, I knew Cameron was visiting the beach house when I dropped you off this morning."

She peered up at me full of understanding.

This was my doing.

I'd pushed Mia away, turned on my asshole nature and not let her in, not allowed myself to really surrender to her, to what we could have been. My inability to give her what she needed had sent her into the arms of my best friend.

"Mia, I need you to know I wouldn't have left you alone. I knew Cameron would take good care of you."

That seemed to comfort her and she smiled and turned, starting toward the glass bay window.

Cameron looked devastated and I couldn't bear to see him like this. "Quite the view."

"Richard, I'm so sorry," his voice broke.

I smirked. "Right to the point."

"I fucked up—"

"That bracelet told me everything I needed to know. I knew you'd fallen hard for her but that proved it beyond all doubt."

"You weren't meant to see what was inscribed on it."

"Yeah, well, I did."

"You gave her up for me?"

"Nothing's changed, Cam. I'll always love her. Always love you, too, you stupid bastard." I gulped my beer to loosen the tightness in my throat. "That doesn't stop me from wanting to shove my fist through your devilishly handsome face."

"Can't blame you."

"Halfway through her training, I realized how she felt about you. It was the way she looked at you...and you her. That time I'd snuck into Chrysalis to visit her, the chemistry between you both was off the charts. I'd hoped it was temporary."

"This was not my intention."

"Promise me you'll take care of her. Don't hurt her, Cam."

"Of course not. Mia's my priority now. Over everything."

"She really broke through to you, didn't she?"

His gaze searched for Mia. She was shoving a canapé in her face, as though trying to comfort herself. Seeing me again so soon was just as hard for her, too, apparently.

Her blonde locks looked ruffled from the breeze, her mouth pouty and petulant.

"You can't tame her, Cam. You know that, right?" I mused out loud.

"It's fun trying."

"She's so infuriating. Which means she's perfect for you."

Cameron looked worried and it made me smile.

"She'll be fine."

He turned back to face me. "How about you, buddy? How are you doing?"

"Well, wouldn't mind a session with you. Help me dig out this ex-cruciating pain in my heart."

"Richard, I—"

"Have you ever considered that I want you to be happy, too? That despite all this confusion, there's actually a good outcome."

"I'll make it up to you."

"Just stop interfering in my life, okay?"

"I really did mean for this to work. For you and Mia—"

"Arrogant fuck."

I leaned into his embrace not caring if anyone noticed our affection. This was the man who'd saved my life too many times to mention, and I wanted him to be happy even more than I wanted happiness for myself.

My thoughts drifted back to Andrea.

She felt like a goddamned dream, softening the edge of angst. The way she looked at me, her voice low and husky. If she ever got into BDSM seriously she'd make a stunning sub with her desire to please. The ease with which she obeyed made me realize she'd be relatively easy to train.

In comparison, Mia had been a goddamned car wreck.

Only with Cameron's expertise had she found her way. Despite having to admit it they really were perfect for each other.

Cameron's stare was fixed on me.

"This is a nice house," I said, trying to break the tension.

"How did you pull off an invite?"

"I was packing my stuff for a jump and debating whether to use a parachute," I said, grinning, "when I got a call from Andrea Buckingham's personal assistant inviting me here tonight."

"Just like that? Out of the blue?"

"We met briefly at a charity event I attended with Hope. Andrea had an entourage and we didn't talk for long. Didn't think she'd remember me."

"You're very memorable."

"Not sure how they got my number. I was too surprised to ask. Andrea's around here somewhere."

If she's roused from her post-climax nap.

It made me smile. "I'll introduce you. Tell her you're my plus one so you don't get kicked out." I laughed. "Might just drink her beer and take a dip in her pool. No doubt Mia will be in there by the end of the night."

"Where's our host now?"

I shook my head as though unsure. "Andrea summoned me into her office to talk privately."

"About?"

"She wants to research BDSM for a role."

Cameron looked amused. "And how did she find out you're connected to Enthrall?"

"Through a friend of a friend, apparently. I'll find out who and ban the bastard."

Of course that would never happen and Cameron didn't need to know it was Ethan. I wasn't in the mood to explain just what Andrea was asking of me. I didn't want to hear training her was a bad idea.

"What did you tell her?" he said.

"For a woman who's used to getting whatever she wants, I left her shell-shocked. Her assistant Sienna's more my type. Pure sub material."

Cameron squinted my way and something told me he didn't believe my attempt to throw him off the scent of my impending adventure.

"Sounds intriguing."

"Mia will be fine," I said, trying to distract him. "She can look after herself."

"Sure." He threw back his champagne.

"Let's go find her."

"Probably a good idea."

He made me smile.

We headed on into the house and went in search of Mia. Cameron's cool demeanor was lost as we moved from room to room.

Another highlight of tonight was watching Cameron's expression go from concern to mischief as he pulled out his phone and scrolled through the screen.

He texted her.

It was unlike Mia not to respond and we shared a concerned glance.

"Fuck it," he said.

I peered over his shoulder. "Something wrong?"

Cameron slid the page to the right and up popped a small red dot. The bastard had a tracking device on her.

I rolled my eyes. "Seriously?"

"Don't judge me." He waved his phone. "Comes in handy for moments like this."

Following him, we made our way up the staircase and down a hallway, me muttering to Cameron about what a complete stalker he was and him ignoring me.

He knocked on a door.

I peered back down the hallway, nervous that Andrea might catch us exploring and question our motives.

We stepped inside a room with a queen-sized bed in the middle, along with a lone dress and a couple of landscape paintings - and not much else.

My gaze fell back on his phone. "Is that thing right?"

He strolled over to the closet door and yanked it open - revealing Mia standing inside, her arms crossed.

"Cameron!" she snapped. "Did you stick a bug up my ass when I was sleeping?"

I laughed at her cuteness.

"Please be more selective with your choice of words," he scolded, shoving his phone in his jacket pocket.

She narrowed her gaze. "Then how did you find me?"

"Why are you in here?"

"Mia," I said. "Don't let these people intimidate you."

"I'm not intimidated."

"Good."

Cameron glared at me as though rattled by just how much I was getting a kick out of this. Seriously, even the great Cameron Cole couldn't tame this one.

"Mia, he's not handing you back to me," I said.

She twisted her mouth petulantly. "Where's the bug, Cameron?"

"It's the magic of love. I felt your presence and—"

"Cameron," she snapped.

"Enough of this."

She rested her hands on her hips. "I knew it."

Cameron's back stiffened. "Mia, trust me, a man in my position—"

"Is it in my shoe?"

"One more word and I'll forbid you to speak for the rest of the evening."

"Seriously, Mia," I said, "we were looking forward to the *hors d'oeuvres* you went to get us."

"She who cannot be named is here," Mia blurted out. "I needed a moment."

"What?" I swapped a wary glance with her. "McKenzie Carlton?"

"She must have seen us arrive," said Mia. "Because McKenzie took me aside and told me who she was."

"You two talked?" Cam's voice sounded strained.

"Yes."

"What about?" I said.

"Out of there," he snapped. "Now."

Mia's face flushed and she hurried out, nearing Cameron and staring up at his usual stance, her gaze full of obedience, respectful of his command.

"Let's go find Zie," I said with a grin.

Cameron shot me a glare.

I gave a shrug. "Or not."

"How about this?" he said, "Let's see the new year in somewhere more…"

I arched a brow. "Your place then?"

"I'd like that," said Mia.

And I imagined Cameron had noticed her aroused state triggered by his commanding presence, her nipples hard and nudging the material.

Turning quick on my heels, I spun round and made my way out.

Cameron and Mia stayed close behind me.

Other guests were blocking the stairs, and we politely asked them to move so we could pass them. The sound of rock music surrounded us, voices raised to speak over the noise, and someone, somewhere, let off a party popper.

I led us toward the exit, psyching myself for the photogs.

I sensed Cameron was no longer behind me and made my way back to see why he'd stopped suddenly.

He'd been trapped by McKenzie Carlton, his expression one of forced politeness. Mia stood behind Cameron as though using him as a human shield.

Yep, Zie had that effect on anyone who knew her well. Cameron's ex-fiancée was back in town, apparently, and already haunting him.

"Nice to see you, too, Cam." McKenzie flashed a dazzling white smile over his shoulder. "Hello again, Mia. I so enjoyed our little chat. Very informative." She could see Mia was wary of her and this seemed to inflame her pride.

Mia's fingers curled around Cameron's hand and he glance back with a comforting smile - which seemed to rattle Zie.

"Richard," she said, "you still working at that place?"

"Yes, if you're referring to Enthrall." I raised my voice to retaliate. "How's the upper east side? All the happier for you not being there, I imagine."

"We were just leaving," said Cameron, gesturing to me.

"Congrats on your engagement," said McKenzie.

Cameron merely smiled back, unfazed.

"Willow broke the news," added Zie. "We had coffee last week. She didn't mention seeing me?"

"No, we haven't spoken recently."

"I'd heard through the grapevine that Mia was your submissive, Richard."

"How do you know Andrea?" I asked, feeling protective of her.

"Through Megan Banks. She's Andrea's publicist. Megan and I were in the same sorority."

It made me wonder what kind of people Andrea surrounded herself with.

I sensed her before I saw her.

Through the many faces in the crowd, I caught Andrea chatting with friends. She beamed over at me and I grinned back, struck by her beauty all over again...her warm chestnut brown eyes, that cute, freckled button nose. Her beauty drew the attention of everyone around her.

My cheeks flushed as I recalled what she and I had gotten up to not that long ago. Her perfume still lingered on me.

I regretted not finding out how she tasted.

She pressed her fingertips to her lips, as though she too was remembering how I'd kissed her. Our passion threatened to burn me alive.

A crowd stepped between us and the moment was lost.

I'd been holding my breath.

I needed to be grounded and not allow myself to be pulled into this vortex.

McKenzie's terseness drew me back—

"I wore it for you in the end, remember? You were very persuasive. I loved that about you."

Cameron turned to face Mia. "Different choker."

McKenzie did that thing with her mouth, sliding the tip of her tongue suggestively along her upper lip.

"Well, this has been delightful." Cameron ran his fingers through his hair. "But if you'll excuse us, we have somewhere to be."

"Cameron." Zie tried to pull him back. "We need to talk."

His face showed the pain he was feeling.

"Hey, buddy," I said, patting his back.

"I'm sorry, what about?" he muttered.

"It's personal."

He stepped back. "Not a good idea."

I gave his arm a tug. "We're gonna be late."

Cameron tapped Zie's arm with affection. "Another time perhaps?"

"I have an appointment to see you."

"At my office?" he said. "I'll book you in with Dr. Laura Raul. She's more—"

"I've been seeing Laura. She believes an appointment with you will bring closure."

I didn't know how Cameron dealt with such fragile people all the time, guiding them through sessions that inevitably healed them but no doubt left a toll on him.

"McKenzie, have a lovely evening," Cameron said, then guided Mia out.

I threw McKenzie a wave and followed them.

The photographers were all over some young actor who'd pulled up in a Veritas RS III, and who'd just thrown the keys to a worried looking valet.

I waved at Leo, Cameron's driver, but he'd already spotted us coming out. All three of us scrambled into the back of Cameron's long black limo.

"I need a fucking drink." I flopped into the leather seat and reached over for that chilled bottle of Bollinger resting on ice. Mia gathered three crystal flutes.

Cameron looked grey.

Mia held out the glasses and I poured champagne into each one. Mia handed one to Cameron and then took a sip from hers.

"Good girl," I said, and threw mine back.

I'd never seen Mia so uncertain, and it was too painful to see. I broke my gaze from hers and stared at Cameron, silently messaging him to say something to reassure her.

"Well, that was unexpected," was all he managed.

"She still loves you," whispered Mia.

Cameron flinched.

I raised my drink in a toast. "Happy New Year!"

He forced a smile.

Zie Carter had hurt Cameron so badly that it was only now that I realized he, too, had doubted he'd ever love again. Giving Mia up to him had probably saved him. I wondered if Cameron knew how much he truly loved her.

One thing was certain: Zie Carter was back in town and from here on in we'd have to watch our backs.

CHAPTER 7

I TOOK AN Uber home.

I could have had Chrysalis's official driver pick me up from Cameron's, but I'd spent New Year's Eve drinking with him.

Cam had invited Leo, myself, and Mia back to his place for a late night soiree after Andrea Buckingham's party had gone south when Zie had turned up.

Too tipsy to drive home, I'd shacked up for the night in one of Cam's guest bedrooms. Leo had promised to retrieve my car from Doheny Drive.

I had no plans on ever going back.

Oh no...

I vaguely remembered sweeping up Andrea in a whirl of passion and inappropriateness for a first meeting. *That's right*, my addled brain caught up, *she wants to be your sub for a few weeks.* Or perhaps I'd dreamt that in a haze of *Piper-Heidsieck* Champagne that I'd quaffed a little too much of last night.

What was post-asshole etiquette? Sending flowers? A note? A phone call? Hell, chances are I'd never get put through to her phone.

I scrolled through mine and caught sight of my conversation sent via text to Andrea last night while partying at Cam's house.

My frown deepened.

Reading my messages, I saw I'd delivered a virtual spanking to Andrea, apparently. That would be the last time I'd hear from her then.

I really was fucking up in all departments.

Note to self: Hanging out with bestie and his new girlfriend - who used to be my girlfriend? Bad idea.

My lingering hangover worsened.

Closing the front door behind me, I heard Winston's paws patting toward me.

That familiar sound of home - my dog's toenails tearing along the hardwood floors.

My English bulldog made sure I never felt consumed by the vastness of my four bedroom home in Malibu. Its generous living room had a long glass wall overlooking the pool, and beyond the well-tended garden lay a path that led down to the golden sandy beach - that rejuvenating ocean a minute's walk away.

Memories of Mia flooded in.

I shook my head to clear them.

At nine in the morning the brightness of the place was blinding, and though I'd had enough time to sober up, I still needed my sunglasses. An ocean-sized ice-cold glass of lemon-water, pancakes, coffee and a morning swim would clear my head.

I beat Winston to the kitchen, only to hear his paws do a 180, as he turned the corner fast and leaped into my lap. I nuzzled against his silly face and ran my hands up and down his fur.

"Hey, Winnie." I laughed at his enthusiasm.

Most owners would never be able to leave their pet alone when fireworks were set to light up the night sky, but nothing bothered my goofy mutt. He merely napped soundly until I got home.

I felt startled when I saw that his water bowl was full. Usually he'd have the thing sucked dry by the time I'd gotten home.

I sprang up.

A young woman stood in the shadows.

What the fuck!

Her black complexion was flawless, her physique pure athlete, her khakis and matching T-shirt suggesting military - her severity only barely softened by her prettiness.

Winston barked. My head pounded with a rush of blood. I reached for my sunglasses to better see, but they flew off and skidded across the floor.

"Hello, sir," said the woman calmly.

"It's okay, buddy," I said, calming Winston.

My body felt frozen - I couldn't move, couldn't run. My mouth stuck shut and my brain flew into overdrive.

Her gaze darted around the kitchen, as though assessing any possible danger.

"Did I scare you, sir?" she whispered, raising her hand to reassure me.

I wanted to say, *"Who the hell are you?"* But I didn't. I forced my expression to remain calm. "Good morning." My heart thundered as I tried to slow my breathing.

A million possibilities ran through my head: she worked for one of my father's enemies and they'd found me? Her family had lost money because of mine? Perhaps I'd stumbled in on a burglary?

She seemed so composed.

Shit. Where were the others?

And how many?

Had she been expecting me?

Her smile was out of place. "I'm Emma." She held out her phone. "Mr. Gardner's on the line. He wants to talk to you."

"You work for him?" My voice sounded strained.

Glancing down at Winston, I suddenly realized with horror that he'd been alone with her in the house.

My hand shook as I grabbed a Smartphone off the counter, doubting the wisdom of closing the gap between us.

I snapped the phone to my ear. "Shay?"

"Hey there, buddy," he clipped back merrily.

"Start talking," I seethed.

"Happy New Year."

He was close to getting a *fuck you.* "Why is there a stranger in my house?"

"Emma works for me. We upped the security while we were in London, remember?"

It was too late to pull back on my frown.

I spun round and faced the wall. "Shay, you speak to me before setting something like this up. I nearly had a goddamned heart attack."

"Sorry about that."

"Next time I see you…"

"Calm down and let me explain—"

"A text would have been nice."

I yanked open the fridge door. Reaching in, I grabbed a bottle of water, twisted the cap open with my teeth and spat out the lid. I gulped down the water like I'd been trapped on a desert island for weeks.

I kept the phone crushed to my ear.

"Are you still there?" said Shay.

"No."

"Cameron gave me the night off. I'm in Santa Monica Harbor, remember? I did invite you. I took the yacht out with Arianna and Henry. How was your evening?"

"Does everyone know where the hell I was tonight?"

"Just me."

"And your team?"

"Obviously."

"Might want to change your business name from CyberVape to Stalkers-Are-Us."

He chuckled. "So how was the party?"

"I want a complete list of all your staff. With photos. By this afternoon."

"Sure."

I glanced warily at the woman. "Did Cameron set this up?"

"No."

"Explain then."

"Is your phone dead?"

"Might be. Might have turned it off so everyone leaves me the fuck alone."

"There was a breech in your security. Emma followed protocol."

"Breech?"

Emma tilted her head toward the hallway that led to the south bedroom, and I followed her gaze.

Andrea Buckingham stood in the doorway - wearing one of my shirts. I assumed she was completely naked under it. She blinked at me as though she'd just woken up.

"She broke in?" I muttered.

"Hi, Richard," said Andrea sheepishly.

"We thought it best to let Andrea stay," said Shay. "She told us you'd be okay with it. Still, we didn't want to leave her unsupervised. Might want to give her a key next time."

"Good to know," I said, feeling dazed.

"Richard," Shay whispered, "how the hell do you have Andrea Buckingham in your bed?"

"Goodbye, Shay." I offered Emma her phone back.

She took it. "So, we're all good, sir?"

"I can handle it from here," I said. "Sorry if I seemed a little—" A tilt of my head said the rest.

"No problem." She gave Andrea a wary glance.

"Emma's promised me her discretion," Andrea called over. "She won't tell anyone I've been here."

"Maybe you could learn a thing or two from Emma," I said dryly. I turned around to thank her, but she was gone.

Winston stared up at me.

"Let's take you outside," I said.

Andrea looked worried.

I patted my leg. "Here, Winston."

"Shall I make you a drink?"

"Stay put. When I get back I'm going to throw you over my lap and I'm going to spank you."

"Not talk first?"

I gave her a look and stormed out.

Winston trotted around the garden taking his time to find the right spot, which gave me time to come up with the best plan. Andrea might have been every man's wet dream, but she'd broken into my home and forced a meeting.

What bothered me more was how my cock didn't seem half as irritated. It was pressing against my pants, firm and willing to be freed like a honing device ready to target that actress pussy waiting for me inside.

This was insanity.

"Spoiled brat," I muttered, leaving Winston in the garden as I stomped toward the hallway.

Andrea wasn't in the bedroom so I moved on to the bathroom.

She sat on the toilet. "I'm having a pee," she said, stating the obvious.

Folding my arms, I leaned on the doorframe.

"Do you mind?" she said.

"This is my house."

"Can't go with you standing there."

"I'm waiting."

"What for?"

"For you to fall to your knees and follow me."

"Very funny. Can we go back to bed?"

"No, sub, we can't."

She pulled several sheets from the toilet roll. "I thought it would be a nice surprise. Didn't think you'd set your guards on me."

"You do realize breaking and entering is illegal?"

"But we're seeing each other now."

"Not like that." I regretted saying it when her face fell.

"Mr. Booth, we have a two week agreement, remember?"

"Like I could forget."

"So I figured it would be okay."

"Not okay, Andrea."

She rose and strolled over to the sink, turned on the faucet and washed her hands. "Your security's pretty tight. I think it might be better than mine."

"We have a great team."

"You and Cameron?"

"The business."

She dried her hands on a towel. "Your clients are high-end?"

"If you're not careful I'll be dropping you off at your cousin's place this morning. The man with the big mouth."

"Ethan?"

"Yes, he should know better."

"He knew I was desperate."

"Well, that makes me feel better." I narrowed my gaze on her. "Have you ever considered acting classes?"

"I'm here because…"

"Go on."

"Ethan told me you do exceptional work at Enthrall."

She looked so fragile and it reminded me why I never took on untrained subs, even if she had stepped out of her comfort zone by risking a break-in and getting caught. The consequences could have included a night in jail and one of those celebrity arrest photos shared by every news outlet.

I ran my fingers through my hair, feeling conflicted.

I had a block when it came to taking on the responsibly of bestowing the right balance of pleasure and pain to an innocent unsure of her own limits - even if Andrea seemed willing to try anything.

She'd tipped her hand by mentioning her aversion to pain and if I was going to extract myself from this precarious agreement this might be the chance I needed. Although I felt curious as to the cause of her subconscious block, I, unlike Cameron, had no interest in diving into her psyche and unleashing the kind of drama I usually avoided.

I'd made a mistake promising to take her on. A glint of light at the end of the escape tunnel appeared, and I settled into the intuitive. It was time to bail.

Push away.

Piss her off and end this debacle.

Hadn't I already tried that once?

"What are you thinking?" she whispered.

"Disobedient subs are always punished."

"You're going to spank me, aren't you?"

"I am."

CHAPTER 8

FRESH BREWED BEANS poured from the coffeemaker into the glass pot.

"You're having coffee first?" said Andrea nervously.

"Apparently."

"We can't get it over with?"

"You make is sound so unappealing."

Her gaze swept the kitchen.

"How did you get in?" I said.

"My bodyguard picked your lock."

"And my alarm?"

"Deactivated it." She shrugged. "He's ex-secret service."

My fingers twitched for my phone to call Shay back.

"Bill has a connection at the security company," she said.

"Bill's your bodyguard?"

She nodded. "He made a call and they turned off your alarm."

"I could sue the lot of you." I ran my hands over my face. "Maybe I'll just hire Bill."

"I'm your consolation prize!"

I leaned back against the kitchen counter. "Do you run?"

She smirked. "Why? Am I going to want to run away from you?"

I smirked back. "You know that high you get when you've hit that fifteen minute mark during a run?"

"Usually kicks in after twenty for me."

"That's the high you get from spanking."

She looked surprised. "I'll like it?"

"Not only will you like it, Andrea, you'll enjoy it so much you'll beg me not to stop." I lifted the pot and poured two coffees, marveling how I was still drinking any Cole beverage after the crap Cameron had pulled lately.

"Is that the case for everyone?"

"Yes. We teach spanking to couples at Enthrall."

"How long have you worked there?"

"Rule Number Two. We never talk about me."

"Why?"

"Because our focus will be entirely on you."

While I spank your pale ass into oblivion.

She narrowed her gaze. "I'm not the kind of woman you think I am."

"And what kind is that?" I handed her a mug.

She wrapped her hands around it. "I've had to claw my way to the top. The competition's fierce. Same with Ethan, he's had to work hard too."

"I know. About the competition, that is."

"And staying at this level—"

"The coveted A-List." I took a sip.

"You make it sound stupid."

"There's a superficiality to it."

"You really don't care for my work, do you?"

"Kind of, sort of."

"What is that supposed to mean?"

"I appreciate acting as a craft. Marlon Brando, Nicholson, Daniel Day-Lewis."

"Any females in there? And don't say Meryl Streep."

"Meryl Streep."

She gave a thin smile. "The publicity is how we maintain our careers."

"You risked bringing the press here. I don't want to have to move after we're done."

"I wore a wig. Bill used his defensive driving technique."

"They could have followed you."

"I have an agreement with my neighbor. They let me use their driveway."

"I'm the spontaneous one," I said. "Moving forward - just so we're clear."

"I promise."

"Ready?"

She grazed her lip with her teeth.

"Stay here," I told Winston and set my mug down, pointing at Andrea. "You follow."

Andrea closed the door on Winston and joined me in the living room.

I headed on over to close the blinds and the room fell dark. A quick scan of the sound system and I chose "Angelicas" by Delirium to set the scene.

Taking a seat on the large leather sofa, I signaled for her to approach. She hugged herself, her cheeks flushed - possibly from both the coffee and the thought of her impending punishment.

She stood before me and let me take her hands.

"Ms. Buckingham, this is how we punish unruly behavior."

"What if I promise never to do it again?"

"That's a given." I yanked her arm forward and she landed squarely over my lap.

Lifting her shirt - my shirt - I ran firm fingers over her buttocks, exploring, and then gave her thong a tweak. It snapped against her flesh and made her jump.

"Twenty minutes," she soothed herself.

"Maybe your high will kick in sooner." I ripped off her thong. "Maybe not."

She gasped.

Running my hands along her spine, I admired her curves, her soft skin, the way she trembled, her short sharp breaths revealing her excitement.

She gave a nod she was ready.

My hand came down sharp and she sucked in a breath.

"Arms behind your back," I demanded, clutching her wrists together.

I peeled off my necktie and used it to secure her wrists.

Centering myself, I readied for her session.

"Your safe word is 'stop,'" I said flatly.

"Won't need it."

Spanking sounds echoed in the room and that slow burn of heat set my palm alight. Each strike leaving a red welt on her butt cheeks, her gasping turning into deep-throated moans of pleasure. I eased her thighs apart, my slaps more gentle as they fell against her sex, causing her to squirm.

Grabbing each cheek, massaging, spanking, my hand sliding between her thighs now and again to provide a brisk stroke there, setting the perfect rhythm until she slipped into subspace, her thighs shaking, her arousal taking her higher.

I realized how hard I was pushing her and even though she softened in my lap, went with the rhythm and seemingly enjoyed it, it dawned on me I'd done the same to my last love Mia, balancing the rawest love and blocking my own heart.

Before me lay the most exquisite creature - a second chance I didn't deserve. Though it wasn't as if there was any kind of future for us, even with this spark of chemistry.

"Thank you, sir," she burst out.

A thrill shot up my spine at the idea of having her here and on my lap. My cock pressed against her stomach, yearning for this moment to never end.

I continued on, trancing out at the sound of these steady slaps, the heat to my palm a rewarding sting. Her skin had reddened in blotches covering her entire butt; heated and sensitive.

This, my favorite penchant - spanking.

Resting my hand on her scorched bottom, I gave her a minute to recover. Then I released her wrists and threw the tie down on the floor.

Andrea shifted and I helped her stand.

She turned and faced me with her head bowed, trembling slightly, her hands held behind her back in a familiar pose that hinted she'd be a natural at this.

Staring up at her, I waited for her to snap...cry...scream at me.

I braced myself for the feel of those red fingernails clawing at my eyes.

I tilted my head, trying to read her.

She brought her hands around and lifted the shirt, her fingers touching her sex, parting her labia, her breaths short and sharp.

She posed like that for me...a breathtaking vision of erotic beauty.

Our eyes met and I fell into her soulful gaze that proved she was desirous of more. My focus lowered to her soaking wet arousal, her fingers parting her swollen labia in a gesture of offering. Her jaw slack, her eyelids heavy, her need burning her up as that tell-tale blush rose on her chest.

"Master," she whispered, her fingertip resting on her clit, beckoning...alluring. "Yours."

In what felt like an out-of-body experience, I moved off the couch and knelt before her, leaning into the beauty of her sex. My mouth met the softest flesh, tasting that first spark of her sweetness as my tongue ran along her clit, exploring, savoring her wetness and questioning why my plan had gone awry...exulting that it had.

There's always tomorrow, I reasoned. We both needed this now - me suckling at the core of this stunning goddess and her deserving a reward for enduring the fiercest punishment.

Andrea's fingers curled through my hair. I grabbed her wrists and with my left hand, positioned them behind her back, holding them together firmly. Tracing her clit with the tip of my tongue, flicking it faster, my own need barely contained as I took her to the edge of pleasure and nudged her over.

Her head fell back and she moaned her climax, shuddering against me, her gasps loud and yearning.

"Oh, please." She sucked in air. "Please."

Delivering the flicking she needed to send her over again, I continued to expertly own her sex with my tongue, feeling the pressure of her as she tilted her hips and pressed herself toward me. Rocking against me now, her body trembling, her head back, her dark locks spilling behind her.

Another orgasm forced her to still...to shudder.

Taking her down slowly, I continued to nuzzle her - kissing, licking, and nurturing.

"This is amazing," she said in a rush.

I smiled up at her. "If you attach pleasure to anything it's bearable."

"I didn't mean that. I meant being here with you."

An inconvenient jolt of happiness spurred me to stand, and I cupped her face with my hands and kissed her mouth; providing her with a sensual tasting of herself from my lips.

Denying myself the urge to take the kiss further, I scooped her in my arms and carried her out of the living room. Andrea rested her head against my chest. We continued on down the hallway until we reached the bedroom. I laid her on the bed and she rested her head on a pillow. I pulled a blanket over her.

The sheets were already ruffled from where she'd fallen asleep earlier. She snuggled beneath the covers. There, on the side table, was that blonde, short wig she'd worn. She also knew how it felt to be forced to hide.

But now she looked so peaceful, so safe, hidden away in my Malibu sanctuary.

I turned to go.

"Lie beside me?" she said.

"I'll make us some breakfast."

"Richard?"

"Yes."

"It kicked in after five minutes."

I paused to take in her meaning.

"My high."

"Oh, good."

My heart broke all over again. A class-A asshole didn't deserve a woman like her.

"Why haven't you taken advantage of me?" she said softly. "Everyone else does."

I felt a jolt of guilt at her naivety. I had, after all, just delivered a high-end series of slaps to an unseasoned sub.

Her eyelids fluttered shut. "You're my master now."

"Go to sleep."

CHAPTER 9

MAKING BREAKFAST FOR Andrea Buckingham felt surreal.

I set about cracking eggs, adding milk, butter, and salt into a pan and whisking the ingredients. Spacing out several times, I nearly burned them in a daze of disbelief. The woman who'd always seemed like an impossible conquest was taking a post-spanked nap in my bed.

Cameron, the one person I'd usually call and share this with was unreachable and probably still in bed with my girlfriend, who he'd claimed as own.

I'd been destined to spend my New Year's Day morning moping around, watching football and talking to Winston, which really was like talking to myself. Yet here I was grinning like an idiot and trying to come to terms with the fact that the stunning brunette who'd captured the hearts of a nation had chosen to be here with me.

I had to remind myself this was merely an extension of our agreement...a temporary contract. If there was one thing I knew for sure it was that I didn't deserve Andrea Buckingham.

I didn't deserve to be happy, period.

I knew this in the marrow of my bones. I'd treated Mia so terribly over the last few weeks, kept her at arm's length for fear of hurting her, breaking her, loving her too much because of that terrifying fear I'd lose her. And as a result Mia no longer lived here. A flood of sadness swept over me, my heart aching, my chest tight with regret.

Winston stared up at me.

"I just fed you," I said. "Look."

He followed my gaze toward his bowl.

"It's in your tummy. You can't pretend you didn't eat it because I watched you scarf it down. Seriously, buddy, what kind of fool do you take me for?"

Winston barked.

"Shush." I pressed my fingers to my lips. "Remember, sleeping beauty."

"Good morning," said a drowsy Andrea from the doorway.

Winston ran toward her.

She knelt and patted him and he wagged his tail, turning around so she could have better access to his lower back.

"You are one cute dog," she said.

"He's a crappy guard dog," I said. "But you've already discovered that. Coffee?"

She pushed herself to her feet. "God, yes, please."

Even while wiping the tiredness from her eyes, she was beautiful, that curvy figure hidden beneath my white shirt, her lustrous locks silhouetted by the daylight streaming in from the window.

"Is it my hair?" She flattened it self-consciously.

I quickly tore my gaze away.

"You're used to seeing me all made up. I know I look ugly in the morning."

"You're gorgeous in the morning." Realizing how that came out I turned away from her. "Breakfast?" I waved the spatula. "Hope you like eggs."

"Love them." She patted barefoot toward me and sat on a barstool, her elbows resting on the central marble counter. She smiled at me sweetly.

I poured two coffees and handed her one.

"Have you forgiven me?"

"You mean for breaking and entering?" I blew on my steaming drink.

"Allegedly."

"You were lucky. All Shay's staff are ex-special forces. She could have taken your ass down."

"My ass has been through enough." She slapped her hand to her mouth. "I meant my butt! My butt has been through enough." She blushed wildly.

She made me smile and my quick retort about how I'd only just begun to worship her pretty little ass seemed out of place. "Let's eat *alfresco*."

We took our coffees and plates with us and settled outside beneath a sun lounger. I went back inside briefly to get a blanket to cover Andrea's legs and ward off the ocean breeze.

I pointed to the end of the garden. "That gate leads to the beach."

She sat back. "Great location. Great house, Richard."

"I like it."

"You live alone?"

I looked down at Winston. "Yes, it's just us."

"Ever get lonely?"

My gaze shot to hers as I considered telling Andrea that twenty-four hours ago I was meant to be heading off for a romantic getaway with my girlfriend. Right up until I'd dropped Mia off at Cameron's beach house. But it was the last thing I wanted to talk about. There'd inevitably be more questions. The most obvious reaction, *what the fuck had I been thinking?*

Second guessing myself, I wondered if there was still time to drive over to Cameron's and beg Mia to come back.

"Are you okay?

"Yeah. How about you?" I said.

"You mean…do I get lonely?"

"Sure, I know you're surrounded by people every day, but still."

"I'm careful who I let get close."

"Very wise."

Before Mia I'd had no woman in my home. After Mia, I'd entertained Hope, my deceased ex-fiancée's twin sister, and even allowed Chrysalis premier submissive and supermodel and wanna-be-actress Jasmine Tate to stay after she'd lost her master during a British scandal. That particular debacle had gone away, thanks to Shay.

Perhaps there really was a genius to Cameron's madness. I'd turned a new leaf and had allowed myself to care again, let those women get close, trusted myself to be strong for them. And though Mia had always suspected I'd slept with Hope and Jasmine, I'd always stayed loyal to her.

"Not the flowers," I called over to Winston.

He peed on them anyway and it made Andrea laugh.

My phone rang from the kitchen. No doubt it was Cameron calling again to check on me - for the hundredth time.

I'm just fine, actually more than fine, I mused. *I'm here with* the *Andrea Buckingham, and no thanks to you and your wily ways the day's looking up.*

"Do you need to get that?" she asked.

"No."

"Ex-girlfriend?"

"No."

"Well, whoever it is sounds like they really need to get a hold of you."

That's because he's riddled with guilt. We all were. Me, for purposefully pushing Mia away, and Cameron for his inability to do so. And Mia, for following her heart.

I scooped another mouthful of eggs onto my fork.

"Ethan told me a little about you." Andrea took a bite of toast.

"What did he say?"

"Not much." She dabbed her mouth with the napkin.

"So you Googled me?" On her nod I added, "Well, now you know why I need to stay out of the public eye."

"You went through so much."

I gave a shrug. "How about you?"

"How do you mean?"

"Tell me more about Andrea Buckingham." I slid my plate away. "Is that your real name?"

"Yes."

"You didn't want a stage name?"

"I was fine with it. Didn't think I'd make it this far to be honest."

"What else would you have done?"

She smirked. "You mean if I'd failed as an actress?"

"I started out studying medicine. Didn't work out."

"Why?"

"I'm better suited to being a stockbroker. I work from home. Have several clients whose accounts I manage. When I'm not at Enthrall."

She gave me a wary look.

"My clients know about my Dad," I said. "Luckily they trust me."

"I trust you." She nudged her plate to the side. "I'd have been a teacher. English, probably. I love children. Do you want children?"

"Never gave it much thought." In truth, I assumed I'd make a crappy dad.

"You have a great collection of books."

My gaze shot to hers.

"Your bookcase."

"Oh, yes."

"You read Geoffrey Chaucer?"

"Yes. And I love anything by Dylan Thomas."

"Me too."

That made me smile. "Are you an Anglophile?"

"I am." She grinned. "Have you ever been to Cornwall?"

"Of course."

"Oh, my God, I'm going to retire in Penzance."

"Mousehole?"

"Yes, I love it there, too." She laughed. "Who knew that a place called Mousehole even existed?"

We shot off all the places we'd visited and I was amazed she even knew of them.

"Do you like Shakespeare?" I said.

"Yes, of course. Theatre is where an actor forges respect." She paused for a moment. "You go by Booth now? You dropped the Sheppard?"

I gave a nod.

"You're from New York?"

"Manhattan. You?"

"Grew up in Florida. Palm Beach. Later, we moved to Michigan."

Which was exactly what my research had turned up after I'd Googled her back at Cameron's last night on my iPhone - though the article had been about her father, a renowned author and celebrity in his own right. Andrea came from money, which meant she was used to getting her own way.

"I'm sorry about what happened to your fiancée," she said softly.

My gaze fell on Winston, my thoughts drifting.

Emily floating in a blood-tinged tub of water after slitting her wrists. Me failing to resuscitate her. Our New York penthouse filled with strangers.

A nightmare never ending.

I sipped my coffee to ease the tightness in my throat.

My fiancée had been just one of the thousands of victims my father had left in his wake. Cameron had saved the day. Saved me. He'd told me time and time again it wasn't my fault. Yet the jury was still out on how far I'd risen on the evil bastard scale.

Andrea's calm presence soothed me; her ethereal beauty enchanting. She'd cracked my defenses.

A jolt of regret that I'd allowed the conversation to derail. "Perhaps it's best we maintain this as a professional relationship?"

"Sorry, I didn't mean—"

"Let's keep our private lives private."

"From each other?"

I gave a comforting smile. "No, from Winston."

She burst out laughing.

"Perhaps it's the best way to protect you from me."

She frowned.

"My family's scandal," I explained.

"That seems like such a long time ago now."

Yet it clung to me with the weight of a fallen son. As though I, too, shared the guilt for all those hurting people who lost their pensions, their savings, and their homes.

"What shows do you watch? And don't say yours." I broke the tension with a smile.

She sat back. "I love *Doctor Who*."

"Seriously?"

"I binge watch it sometimes."

"I love it, too."

"Really?"

"Yes. When I get time."

She grinned so wide I couldn't help but shake my head in response to her cuteness.

"I'm sorry I broke into your house."

I narrowed my gaze. "Don't do it again."

A seagull flew overhead and we watched until it disappeared from view.

"So, we'll meet at Enthrall for sessions?" she said.

"I'll have a dominatrix meet you and escort you through another door."

Andrea's gaze snapped back to me.

"We're connected to a luxury travel office. The manger is a member of Enthrall. We use her facility for certain clients."

"What about Chrysalis?"

"You'll never see the inside of Chrysalis."

"Can't you pull some strings?"

"You mean with myself?"

"You run it?"

"You'll have the privilege of visiting Enthrall. And Enthrall only."

"Scared I might see someone I recognize?"

"Yes. And, as you've proven, you have no tact."

"I do."

I gave her a look.

"Didn't think you'd mind." She pushed her chair back and rose. "Most people are happy to see me."

"I'm not most people."

She strolled away and leaned over the edge of the pool. "When does your pool boy come?"

"Don't have one," I called over. "I take care of it."

Her gaze swept over the house, probably wondering why a millionaire cleaned his own pool.

"I find it cathartic," I said. "Skimming leaves. Adding chlorine. Fixing the tiles."

"Fixing tiles?"

"Yes."

She pointed to the water. "Well, I'd like to take my morning swim. So, if you don't mind, can you pull out those leaves?"

I followed her gaze and saw a few floating in the pool. "Swim around them."

"What if I bump into one?"

I rose and strolled over to her.

"They're kind of icky."

"You're kidding?"

"No, I'm quite serious."

I went on over and grabbed the net off the side of the wall and took a few minutes to scoop them out.

I counted ten. "Happy now?"

"There's still one there." She pointed.

Frowning at her, the word *princess* resting on the tip of my tongue, I swept the net into the center and scooped out the offending leaf. With it safely on dry land and tossed in the corner trash bin, I turned to give her a *there you go* smile.

A breeze came through, rustling the oak tree at the end of the garden. It let go of a single leaf, which rose and was carried across the garden, spiraling onto the water.

Andrea arched a brow.

I threw down the net and approached her. Scooping her up in my arms, I leaned over the pool and threw her in.

She rose to the surface, splashing and spluttering in the water.

"Would you do me a favor?" I called over. "Can you reach that leaf?"

"Not funny," she snapped. "I wasn't planning on getting my hair wet."

"You're joking?"

She swam backwards. "No."

"Feel the same way about my shirt."

Though with the material transparent now it clung to her beautifully, following her curves and hiding nothing as it molded over her pert breasts. She huffed as she pulled it off, ripping buttons, her expression full of annoyance.

It landed in a squelch at my feet.

"You just ripped the buttons off my favorite shirt," I said.

"You have a hundred in there. Anyway, it was icky and wet."

Her breasts rose above the surface, her nipples pert from the morning chill.

"You have an issue with dirty, messy things, don't you?" I said with a smirk.

"I like order. I don't like to be surprised. I like everything clean and—

I dived in and swam toward her.

She narrowed her gaze on me, her hands swirling around her for balance.

Treading water in front of her, I said. "You were saying?"

"Sorry about your shirt."

I grinned. "Could say the same about your hair but this wet puppy look you've got going on is adorable."

"Someone forgot to take off their clothes."

"Being spontaneous is actually healthy. You should try it some time." I unbuttoned my shirt and pulled it off.

"I was spontaneous last night."

"That's right. You're the wanton criminal who broke into my home."

"There were mitigating circumstances."

"In what way?"

"I thought you might change your mind about our agreement."

"Why?"

"Because your signature was illegible. Just a couple of swirls."

"That's the way I sign my name."

"I told Sienna to call you Mr. Sheppard because I knew it would get your attention."

"You knew it would come over as a threat."

"I didn't mean it too." She looked sheepish. "You're a complex man."

"Is that what Ethan told you?"

"He wanted me to know about your past."

"So you knew what you were getting yourself into."

"In case it ever came out we were friends."

"You mean like father, like son?"

"I don't believe that about you. Anyway, Ethan told me you're very kind. You have a healing side."

I was sure Ethan hid the true details of how he'd come to know about my healing touch. Particularly as the truth of it would reveal so much more about her cousin.

"Ethan also told me you'd say no, probably."

I gave a thin smile. "He's right."

She looked devastated.

I owed Ethan. He was, after all, one of us. He protected Chrysalis with the fierceness of a brilliant D.A. who knew the law well, and worked with Dominic to ensure our continued integrity.

"Why are you so reluctant to take me on?" she said.

"Because your motives are not authentic."

"How do you mean?"

"Something else is going on."

"I believe I'll also grow from this experience."

"How?"

She broke my gaze. "Can it be my secret?"

"We shouldn't keep secrets from each other."

"Then I'll tell you. It's so that I feel more comfortable with my body."

And yet she'd lain herself out for me on that desk the first day we'd met, sprawled like a wanton kitten; a woman who was in touch with her sexuality and seemed to like nothing more than coming.

"We shouldn't lie to each other either," I said.

She looked defeated.

"You don't really understand what a submissive is. What I'll do to you."

"You want me to give up control in the bedroom?"

"Not just in the bedroom."

"What else?"

I wrapped my hand around her throat. "Your homework is to recite to me during your first session all the ways a good sub serves her master, understand?"

"Yes," she burst out breathlessly.

"If at any time I see you fight for dominance our agreement will be over."

"Why would I?"

"Because you're used to getting your own way, Andrea. You're spoiled. What you want you get. Proof in point, you're in my pool."

"You're the lucky one."

"Really, is that right?"

She relented and gave a sweet smile.

"The first time I met you we discussed your experience with orgasms."

She raised her chin petulantly.

"That look, right there, is disobedience. I don't tolerate insubordination."

Her lips trembled with excitement.

"From the moment I first saw you I knew you'd make an honorable sub. Don't fight it though. Resist it and you resist me. I don't train subs. Never have. So our agreement is a real privilege for you. Don't take it for granted."

"I don't."

"I'm going to promise you this, Andrea - I'm going to take you to the very limits of pleasure. I'm going to own your body and set every cell on fire with passion. When you're not with me all you'll think about is how well I know your pussy, how exquisitely I play with it, how it tingles when you think of me. You'll come in your dreams, and you'll come as you wake up because where I'm going to take you will burrow so deep inside your psyche you'll never forget what I made you feel—

She'd slipped into subspace.

"I will teach you to come properly. Submit to me and I'll have you climaxing so hard you'll not only forget your own name you'll experience Samadhi."

"What is that?"

"Oneness."

Her eyes opened in wonder.

I lowered my hand in the water and flicked her clit hard, making her yelp.

Her jaw slackened as she rode the buzz of pleasure between her thighs, her quick clit orgasm making her moan.

"Was that nice?" I said huskily.

"Yes, sir."

"Proof that your clit is mine."

"Oh, God." She jolted her hips forward as her body flinched from another spasm in her sex that came back around. "That's not possible."

"Clearly it is."

She looked down at herself in disbelief at what I'd accomplished.

"Now imagine an hour's session with me."

"Master," she whispered.

"Better."

"Sir, thank you for not throwing me out."

I still couldn't quite believe she'd chosen to be here on New Year's Day with me. I was sure her entourage was reeling without her.

"Looks like I'm taking you on."

She threw her head back in a laugh. "It's going to be amazing."

I grinned at her.

"How do you do that?"

I slid out of my pants. "Do what?" The rest of my clothes sank.

"Make me feel so normal?"

"You are."

"No, I mean you make me feel like you like being here with me, for me. Myself."

"I've never cared for fame, or anything ego-based for that matter." I arched a brow. "As far as I'm concerned, you're just like any other submissive whose trust I have to earn."

"But I don't want to be like any other submissive."

"Well, of course I'll make you feel special."

"Is it safe?"

"Yes, I'll never use unnecessary force—"

"No, I mean is it safe for our hearts?"

"We have ways to make the exit easier."

"You mean when our agreement is over?"

"Yes."

"How?"

"Trade secret."

"You'll be cruel to me?"

"What are you looking for, Andrea?"

"I need to be convincing."

"In your role?"

"Yes."

"Then that is what I'll do. I'll teach you all the skills necessary."

She looked around her, realizing her back was pressed against the pool edge and as I leaned against her she wrapped her legs around my waist. My cock pressed into her lower abdomen.

Her gaze fell to my lips. "Is this one of the skills?"

"One of them, yes. As my sub I have access to your pussy at all times. You consent to my cock being inside you day or night - should I choose to take you."

"You'll fuck me any time you like?"

I eased her thighs apart and buried my cock deep inside her. "Yes."

Her head fell back and she thrust her hips forward. "You make me feel…"

"So wet?"

Her muscles gripped me tight and it made my balls thrum.

She let out a sigh. "No, I mean, yes…"

I pounded rhythmically inside her.

"I feel...Oh God...so good..."

I bit her lower lip and her mouth opened wide, allowing my kiss to control hers, possessing her completely.

"I feel like I'm drowning."

I wrapped my arm around her waist. "I've got you."

Andrea's moans entered my mouth as I fucked hers with my tongue, my cock delivering violent strikes, her slickness perfect for these deep plunges. The tension in my erection flooding to the tip as it struck her cervix.

She dug her fingernails into my back. "Harder, Master, fuck me harder."

I gave her what she wanted, needed, taking her like I already owned her, her raw groans turning into primal screams.

"I'm close, Richard."

"I know." I bit her earlobe, suckling her earring.

She pulled back and stared into my eyes. "Promise if I submit the way you want me to you'll not let me drown."

Never.

My cock ached for release but I kept my vow to master her and ignored it, concentrating on hers, making her shiver as she neared climax by playing with her nipples, the left and then the right, pinching, tweaking and when I could resist no longer my mouth took possession of her breasts in turn - sucking, licking, elongating and flicking the pert buds.

I lifted my gaze to drink in her beauty - the impossible hallucination of a madman, this striking creature writhing in my arms?

"What?" she whispered, looking crestfallen that I'd stopped.

I spanked her ass. "Always my way."

With my arms on her hips I spun her around to face the tile. Her back was now to my front, her hands gripping the pool ledge and her knuckles white. Thighs trembling as she arched her spine back and rubbed her butt against my groin, begging with her twisting hips for me to reenter her.

Water lapped around us.

Her craving made her wild; her widening thighs proving her yearning.

Propelling my hips forward I drove back into her.

"Yes!" She fell against the edge.

Forcing through the resistance of water, I delivered slow steady thrusts, my muscles taut with tension, my desire burning me up.

That lone leaf bobbed by, and though her gaze caught it, she no longer cared.

I reached around her waist and my hand slid down to her sex. I flicked her clit in time with my pummeling.

Her yell made my cock spill its pre-cum inside her.

"Andrea, I solemnly swear to teach you how to breathe underwater." I strummed her slowly now, circling, applying more pressure. "Now, come for me. Come hard and prove to me you're mine."

She climaxed - screaming my name.

CHAPTER 10

THREE DAYS.

Three long days since I'd seen Andrea.

A slow-burn approach was best, nothing too drawn out. Short, sharp intensive sessions so she got what she needed from her experience and she and I could remain professional.

The chaotic dance beat pulled me back and my gaze rose to take in the high ceiling of The Manor, its impressive light display almost blinding. We had a great view of the dance floor from our private VIP section and the booze flowed.

But I wasn't drinking tonight. A late night session neared. Andrea had entered my life in a whirl of wild spontaneity and I couldn't wait to truly show her the scene.

Perhaps, I mused, I was subconsciously protecting myself from her. Andrea had a way about her that could render a man useless if he didn't guard his heart. I couldn't cope with another romantic disaster. Keeping my subs at arm's length was a specialty of mine and there was no need to break that habit now.

Just this morning her signed submissive's contract had been personally delivered to Enthrall by Sienna. Her shy assistant had handed that sealed envelope over to me in my office and then scurried away as though I might spank her.

Our world - a hedonistic palace of pleasure - would always be a mystery to those on the outside. The true value of what we did at Enthrall was a well-kept secret.

Arianna, Shay's girlfriend and submissive, was here, as was Scarlet, Lotte, and Penny, who'd brought her husband Miles. He sat in the corner sipping a Martini, seemingly content with people watching.

I'd looked forward to celebrating Scarlet's birthday, and I also had some fantastic news to give Cameron, after spending the day working on his financial portfolio. But it also meant he and Mia might soon turn up their PDA. I wasn't ready for that.

My heart and mind was still reeling from losing my girlfriend.

I'd thrown myself into projects at Enthrall and had dedicated the last few days going over the designs for a new playroom. The lavish dungeon with its deep reds, the finest Italian leathers, and state of the art chrome equipment was coming together perfectly.

I tried not to dwell on that other unobtainable beauty in my life and it was working pretty well, right up until that music video came on the big club screen and lit up the dance floor. Andrea Buckingham's face stared down with her big brown eyes full of wonder, as band member Dillon Rave dragged her over to ride on the back of his Harley.

"Damn, that girl's pretty," said Scarlet, staring at up the screen.

I was shaken out of my melancholy trance.

Both of us continued to watch the drama unfolding - Andrea storming away from Dillon after having her heart broken, apparently, and him now acting out his regret, his deep base retelling the story of what an idiot he'd been and his hope of winning her back.

A pang of jealousy hit me and morphed into a strange pride that the real Andrea was mine for a few weeks.

Shay nudged my arm, his head tilting toward the screen, his expression incredulous. He'd promised to be discreet and not mention Andrea turning up at my place out of the blue. Cameron was too distracted to catch all this. He sat across from us, a laser sharp stare locked on his target, which was Mia on the dance floor.

Arianna danced close to Mia and emerging out of the crowd was Emma, Shay's pretty security guard. It dawned on me why she was a great addition to his team. She'd mingle easily with our women and could go into places we couldn't.

Cameron's all seeing stare found Emma as she danced near the girls and her body language, though discreet, had been picked up by this master of perception. Cameron had never met her either apparently, from the way he swapped a wary glance with Shay.

Shay called over to him. "Ex-special forces. Emma kicks ass."

"Good to know," he said, smiling. "Don't let her kick mine."

I moved closer to Shay and took advantage of the loud music and Cameron being distracted as he texted away.

"I've been hired to train a new submissive," I said, keeping my voice low. "Might want to alert your team the individual's a public figure."

His gaze snapped up to the screen. "There's a risk of discovery."

"We won't go near Chrysalis," I said. "All sessions will be held at Enthrall."

"You can't drive yourself from here on in until the sessions end."

"What?"

"If the press sees you with her and tags your license plate number you're screwed, Richard."

I looked away from him.

"It's my job to protect you." Shay's glare landed on Cameron. "Does he know?"

"Not yet."

The screen lit up flashes of light falling on a laughing Andrea, her hair tumbling over her face, that familiar pouty grin filling the screen.

There were risks when entertaining celebrity clients and Cameron always had the final say on whether they were allowed to enter our elite domain.

"Keep this private for now," I told Shay. "It'll be over in a couple of weeks."

He narrowed his gaze. "Don't go rogue."

"I won't."

"We've worked hard at hiding you away. Don't fuck it up."

"We won't be seen in public."

"I'll implement the protocol."

I cursed the protocol and having never been subject to it before I'd always been grateful I'd avoided it. The idea of a crack squad of security officers tracking my every move made my skin crawl.

"Tell the director," said Shay.

I glanced over at Cameron. "He has a lot on his mind right now."

"When's your first session with Buckingham?"

I shrugged. "Next week."

"Lying bastard." He pushed himself to his feet and towered over me as though trying to grapple for alpha status.

"What's the worst that can happen?" I said flatly.

"I'm upping the security at Enthrall." He wandered over to Cameron.

Glaring at him, I watched to see if he was about to break my trust.

Scarlet plopped down beside me and nuzzled into my arm. "You doing okay, my darling?"

"Why wouldn't I be?"

She stared into my eyes. "My office door is always open."

"Mine too."

"You seem to be taking it well—" She nodded toward Cameron, who was deep in conversation with Shay.

I caught the words Beverly Hills and something about a security camera and relaxed a little when I realized they weren't talking about me.

"Cameron's besotted with Mia." She sighed deeply.

"I've never seen him so happy," I said. "He's my best friend and I owe him this."

"You don't owe him anything."

"I do, Scarlet. We all do. He's saved us all one way or another."

She shrugged her resignation. "You'll be snapped up again in no time."

"I'm saving myself for you, Scar," I said playfully.

She rested her head against my arm. "I love you, Richard Booth Sheppard."

I leaned over and kissed her. "I have to chat with the director."

Scarlet leaned back and ruffled my hair.

I nudged her hand off playfully. "Not the hair." Beaming at her, I rose and headed over to sit beside Cameron.

I gave his back a pat. "Got a second?"

"Of course."

We moved the short distance over to a more private section.

I felt Shay's glare on me and ignored it.

I turned to Cameron. "You look good."

"You too. How are you?"

From the dance floor Mia and Arianna threw us waves.

I waved back.

Cameron looked frazzled.

"You know I love you, right?" I hoped to reassure him. "We miss you at Enthrall."

"We?"

"Me."

"Well, that's good."

"I'm having a party at my place next weekend. Shay, Henry, you, and me."

"You're on."

Beaming at him I watched his expression, assuming he thought I was about to lay a ton of guilt on him. "Cam, when was the last time you checked your shares?"

"I don't know. A week."

"Tripled."

He looked stunned, his gaze staring at the floor trying to process my words.

"Well?"

"Richard, that would make you—"

"A stock-broking genius." A feeling of pride swept over me that I'd managed to triple his portfolio. God knows that was a small miracle after my family's reputation as stockbrokers had been decimated.

"How?"

"An 8% NASDAQ surge." I gave a shrug. "This month saw the highest number of monthly buyback announcements in history."

I went on with the details though Cameron seemed too preoccupied with his thoughts to process the information.

"How can I repay you?" he said.

I slapped his back. "Steak dinner."

He shrugged out of his jacket. The heat was getting to him. Yeah, adding a billion to your stock can do that to a man.

"I'm at a loss for words," he muttered.

"You had faith in me, Cam." I said, staring up at the screen. The vision of a castle now filled the white space, a landscape. "That's reward enough."

His awed expression made me smile.

"What can I tell you, Cam? It's in my blood."

"I'm stunned."

"Maybe now you'll let me dance with your girlfriend?"

"Go have fun," he said. "Thanks again, Richard. I really appreciate what you've done."

I found Mia in the crowd. "She looks happy." I rose to my feet and headed over.

Mia and Arianna welcomed me to the floor as I eased through the crowd to get to them. I flashed a smile at Emma, who gave a discreet nod back. She looked like she could handle pretty much anything and it was reassuring to know Shay had a great team.

I'd not really believed Cameron would let me dance with Mia so soon after our break-up. The undertones of uncertainty still lingered. Mia swayed her hips and glanced warily over at Cameron, who was too busy texting to notice her nervousness.

I leaned into her ear. "One dance and then I'll leave you alone for the evening."

"Don't say it like that," she said. "I'll dance with you anytime you like."

I gave her a crooked smile; we both knew the reality of what we were now. Ours was an awkward friendship that needed time to heal.

We needed *this*.

We danced close, too close, and I questioned the sanity of this decision not least because I wanted to pull her against me, kiss those pouty lips that always felt so good, grind my groin into hers. The music wasn't helping; this rhythmic beat - electric sensuality - was sending the crowd into a writhing frenzy.

I wondered which woman Emma would follow if I split the girls up.

"Let's get a drink," I shouted over the music, grabbing Mia's hand and guiding her through the swaying bodies.

We made it to the long oak bar and I threw a wave at the waiter to get his attention. His gesture told me we were next. Glancing over to our section I saw that Cameron was no longer sitting there.

Feeling mischievous I ordered three shots of tequila.

I leaned low and spoke over the music into Mia's ear. "I'm glad we got this moment to talk."

"I'll always care deeply for you, Richard," she said.

"Cameron's the most incredible man you'll ever have the privilege of dating. Look after him, okay?"

The bartender gave a nod and gestured that he'd add our shots to our table's tab.

My focus returned to Mia. "One for Cameron, too."

"Thank you, Richard."

"For the record, I'd never have let you go had I not liked the man you were leaving me for. Just so you know."

"Please remember it was you who ended us." She broke my gaze as though realizing the ridiculousness of that statement.

I gave her a look of understanding and handed her the small shot glass. "You're happy. Cam's happy. It's a good day."

"What about you?"

I gave a thin smile. "I've survived this far."

She threw the drink back. "I owe you everything, Richard."

"I could say the same."

Her gaze searched for Cameron and she frowned when she couldn't see him.

"Looks like he got a call," I said. "You're going to have to roll with it."

She gave a nod.

"Mia, I didn't always treat you right." I reached out and played with a golden strand of her hair like I always used to.

Realizing how this might look to the others, I withdrew my hand.

"They were challenging times for us all, Richard. I wasn't exactly easy with my emotional block and stuff."

"Please, Mia," I said, "I need to know we're good."

"I'm the one that ended up with your best friend. I'll always be sorry I hurt you—"

I pressed a fingertip to her lips. "Another shot?"

"You didn't drink yours?"

I handed it to her.

She looked at it with caution. "I have to check with Cameron."

"I dare you."

She lifted the glass to her lips and rested it there flirtatiously and then threw it back, her mouth gaping at the burn, that look of pleasure mixed with pain not so dissimilar to those times when I'd thrust my cock deep inside her.

Her face flushed from the liquor.

"There's the Mia I love!"

That blush lit up her neck like a post-fucked glow and it made me smile. I'd be sending her back to Cameron like that with a tell-tale hint of a tryst.

"You look so beautiful," I mouthed, knowing I'd scare her.

"I better go find him."

"Yep."

"Will you be okay?"

I gave a nod and watched her make her way toward the exit. I searched the many faces for Emma, who no doubt would be hot on Mia's heels.

I pulled out my phone and found Andrea's number, sending her a text.

Ready for your first session?

The texting icon flashed away and then came her answer: *Yes, sir.*

My thumbs glided across the screen: *Change of venue.*

We're not meeting at Enthrall?

No. I weaved through the crowd as I texted. *Pendulum.*

CHAPTER 11

"PENDULUM DOESN'T EXIST," I told Andrea as we stood in its dark foyer.

With a flick of my fingertip I turned on the lights. Above us, the multicolored ceiling of glass rained down a reflection of oranges, blues, and delicate hues, complementing the elegant dark wood décor and darker floorboards.

"Oh, my God," she said. "It's beautiful."

"Glass art boutique." I arched a brow.

"We're here to buy glass?"

I grinned at her.

"This is a front?"

"Very good."

"Is this place like Enthrall?"

"Similar, but exclusively for members who can never be seen at Enthrall."

"So if anyone gets caught coming out of here?"

"You were merely perusing the collection of fine Italian glass imported from Europe."

"It's lovely."

"And to view their full collection is by appointment only."

She lowered her gaze. "But of course."

"And no, you don't get to hear who the members are."

"I wasn't going to ask."

"You were."

She giggled and hurried into the center, her head tilted back to view the spectacular display. She spun around, arms out, and shards of light sprayed down prisms upon her.

She stopped suddenly. "Is anyone else here?"

"Only us."

She relaxed again and continued to spin, her dress fanning out, her hair falling over her face as she laughed her joy.

This Manhattan Beach residence sat snugly amongst the other million dollar homes, with its not so regular history, and its remarkable clientele that would make any black book melt.

Reserved only for those in the public eye, its members needed the assurance of solitude and discretion. Politicians, the finest sportsmen, world famous businessmen, all with a lot to lose and therefore this private house served as the finest secret society.

Although I'd never been an official member, my connections saw to it that I had access should I ever want it.

With Andrea's hand in mine I led her along the sweeping hallway.

We paused before the elevator and I punched the button.

"Where does this lead?" she whispered.

"We're alone, Andrea, we can talk normally."

Excitement flushed her cheeks.

Usually a master and his sub would be greeted by a senior dominant, a member of Pendulum, who would remind them of the rules and hand over the keycard to the lowest levels.

I, however, owned a keycard.

I took hold of her left arm firmly and escorted her into the elevator. "This place is unsupervised. Which means I can do anything to you."

The doors slid closed.

She fell into my arms, and nestled her face against my chest, her breathing soft, going with the mood, trusting.

"Let's get you prepared for your session," I said. "Then we'll talk about what you've learned from your homework." I lifted my head back to see her better and said sternly, "You did do your homework?"

"Mostly."

"What does that mean?"

"I read a little."

"And?"

"I wanted to try out a session with full emersion."

Leaning back against the elevator, I felt it jolt to a stop. "Do you know what you're really asking for?"

"Role play?" She bit her lip.

I reached out and traced her mouth with my fingertip. Her tongue flicked out, a sensual act of readiness.

"Very well," I said.

She fell against my chest again in a hug.

"Full emersion means you do what and when I say."

She peered up at me. "I know."

"You will not be entering the lower level of the club on your feet, Andrea. Prepare please."

She fell at my feet, head bowed, trembling.

I knelt before her and tipped her head up. "Do you want to tell me your safe word?"

"I don't...I'm not sure."

"What you're feeling is normal. Anticipation for what's about to happen. Settle into it. I'm not going to promise you I won't push you hard because this is what you're asking of me."

"Yes, I am."

"So, let's begin. Your safe word is?"

"Mercy," she stuttered.

"But I won't be giving you any mercy, Andrea. Choose another."

"Glass."

I rose to my feet, towering over her.

With another slide of the keycard the door opened. I stepped around Andrea and exited the elevator, and gestured she was to follow.

Elegantly, and on all fours, her movements were slow and sure as she crawled after me.

At the end of the hallway before the red door, I ordered her to stand. Exerting total power over my sub too soon during a session would give her time to question and possibly change her mind. I needed to distract her and as she'd no doubt be intrigued with what lay on the other side of that door, this was a good place to start.

With a turn of the handle I gestured she was to go on ahead.

The room appeared simple enough, lavish with its fine Italian leather chairs, complimented by the long studded sofa, the theme of dark wood providing the air of a gentlemen's club, wooden floorboards strewn with Persian rugs. This looked like any regular anteroom, except for the artwork hanging on the walls - historical erotic photos of those who'd indulged in BDSM in the 1800s.

With a wave of my hand, I motioned for her to view them. She walked on ahead and stopped at each one, occasionally glancing back my way.

In the center of the coffee table sat a long wooden box.

From within I removed a studded black diamond collar.

Andrea returned to my side, and went to kneel.

"No, I want you to stand for this."

I left the collar on its box, with light catching those dark jewels and sending a shimmer over the table.

"Time to undress," I said.

She stood still as I unzipped her dress and let it fall to the floor. I unclipped her bra and then pulled down her panties. She stepped out of them to help me. I tucked them into my pocket.

"Next time we meet, no panties," I said.

"Yes," she said nervously. "I mean okay."

I brought the collar over to her and secured it around her neck. The choker looked beautiful on her, a rare antique piece worth millions we'd borrow for the evening.

"Divert your gaze," I whispered.

"Sorry." She glanced at me. "Should I call you Master now?"

"Now would be good, yes." I flicked a stray lock of her hair behind her shoulder. "Stunning."

Her eyelids flicked. "Am I allowed to talk, Master?"

"With permission."

"Okay, sorry."

"I know that surrendering is not easy for you," I soothed. "You're an empowered woman. But let's just say that for one evening you let go, and give your body over to me?" I lifted her chin. "Give yourself to the one man who will worship you completely?"

A noise startled her and she snapped her gaze to mine.

"It's an old house," I said.

"No one's here?"

"No. Just us." I ran my thumb around her areola and she trembled. "Your master's job is to protect you. Security is tight. No one can enter without a key. I have access to the security cameras. The caretaker sweeps for bugs prior to us entering."

She looked surprised.

"Well, this house is designed to entertain presidents. So we take every precaution."

My fingers trailed lower, over her abdomen and slid down to touch her sex. Gently, I eased open her labia and examined her, running a fingertip along her sleekness.

"Good," I said. "Still, I believe what I'm about to show you will inspire you even more."

Her eyelids flickered at my touch.

"You admitted you have a secret?" I said. "Before we proceed any further I need you to tell me what that is."

She shook her head.

"Andrea, keep nothing from me."

"I'm ashamed to say it."

I tugged on her collar and brought her face up to mine. "You will tell me."

She leaned into my ear and whispered it. "I'm afraid, Master, afraid when I wake up in the morning. Afraid of doing the right thing. Afraid of not doing the right thing. I live in fear every day. I know it's irrational. I just can't shake it. Nothing helps."

"Why do you think that is?"

"Because I've been so protected all my life. Maybe that's why? I was always kept out of harm's way."

The downside of privilege; wings so clipped she'd never know what it was like to fly.

"This is the most daring experience I've ever had." She leaned against me. "I'm going to trust this. Trust you."

"Good." I broke her gaze. "When we first met at your party you seemed so confident, so willing to please me?"

"For the first time I didn't need to act. I could just be me."

"With me you are your authentic self?"

"Yes, I promise. I couldn't believe how safe you made me feel. Ethan told me you would."

"Have you tried talking to anyone about this?"

"I've tried everything. You're my last hope, Richard. I tried valium but I can't work when I'm on it." Tears streaked her cheeks, and I wiped them away.

Enthrall had drawn another broken-winged sparrow our way.

My usual instinct was to turn away, give her over to another to heal her, but Andrea needed a breakthrough.

Taking her through this session could very well ease her angst if done right. She'd leave here high on endorphins.

"Widen your thighs a little."

She responded; her breaths short and sharp.

To heal such a subconscious fault line, more thought was needed - a session like no other.

My fingers entered her and I stroked her G-spot.

Her expression mirrored bliss. "Master, don't turn me away, please."

"You must give yourself over to me completely."

"I will."

"Body and soul."

"Yes."

"Very well."

"Thank you, sir."

"I have something very special to show you." I removed my fingers. "This room, everything you see in it was transported from France. Even the wood paneling. And then placed exactly as it had once been in the house of Madame Pen."

"Pendulum?"

"That's right," I said. "The name comes from the private club in Europe and also represents what we do here."

She looked at me, curious.

"Show me." I gestured.

She blushed wildly, her delicate fingers easing apart her labia.

"Remain in that pose, understand?"

She gave a nod.

I strolled on over toward the marble fireplace and on the wall to the right of it, I nudged aside the painting. A flick of a button and a screen lowered from the ceiling.

I pushed another button and from the rear of the room a flickering projector lit up the screen, the black and white film playing out before us.

Andrea's stare locked on the image, her jaw slack, her eyes wide with wonder, her blush wild on her cheeks. She threw a glance at me.

"This was filmed in 1897," I said.

The flickering erotic black and white film shone brightly. A pretty young woman was naked and bound with rope, hanging from the ceiling. She was swinging to and fro. Before her a twenty-something man faced her, dressed in an old-fashioned suit, his jacket long and well-tailored, revealing the elegant fashion of that decade, his pants open at the groin, his erection rearing out of dark curls.

Her swinging stopped.

Standing directly behind her was another man dressed in similar clothes, only his cock was buried deep within the woman now, his hands holding the rope above her and pulling it back so he held her there suspended before him. He let the rope go and the woman swung toward the other man in front of her and he caught the rope and stilled her. As she came to a stop before his groin, her mouth opened to welcome him in, and she sucked furiously, providing that historical blowjob with a French flair. He tilted his hips forward and rocked into her.

Giving her the freedom to work her mouth up and down, the man concentrated on holding the rope, his gaze of affection on her.

After his nod of approval she was let go. She swung back the other way and the man caught her. His cock met her pussy and slid in easily. This time the man holding the rope delivered a series of pelvic thrusts, pounding into her, his face twisted in pleasure.

The woman squirmed and wiggled and, though silent, her screams of orgasm seemed to find us.

"She's the pendulum," whispered Andrea, her hands firmly clutching her labia apart, the erotic tension from holding that pose causing her to tremble uncontrollably.

Taking a few steps toward her I slipped my fingers along her sex. Her wetness soaked my hand.

"You wish that was you?" I whispered.

"Oh, God."

I caressed her highly sensitized clit.

She blushed wildly. "Yes, sir."

I ran a fingertip up and down her, as she continued to watch the scene unfolding. "You're not ready to be shared just yet." I brushed her arm.

"No, sir."

The rope had stilled in the center and both men were taking that femme fatale. She was being fucked hard from behind by one man and her mouth was delivering pleasure to the other.

As the camera pulled back, the view of the room became apparent.

I pointed. "That's where we're going now."

CHAPTER 12

SITTING HIGH ON the throne-like mahogany chair at the end of the long, darkly lit room, I waited.

Andrea was at the other end, near the back table, mulling over which one of the many whips, chains, and toys she should bring me.

I'd spent the last half hour binding her in rope and honoring the art of Shibari. That ancient bondage once reserved for prisoners was now reserved for beloved submissives who deserved the time and effort it took to wrap intricate strands in symmetrical patterns around their naked body.

Andrea looked stunning as she crawled on all fours toward me with that long, thin whip between her teeth - her movements sleek and elegant, her bottom waggling, her expression one of exhilaration.

This was where I was meant to be and this was who I was: A master who knew intuitively what his submissive needed - knew how to guide her into the scene so she felt honored and beautifully feminine, so that she trusted the play and would follow any command.

My cock ached for her.

She was the most exquisite submissive I'd ever had the privilege of playing with; a natural so into the scene that she required minimal training, being a fast learner.

Andrea rose up on her heels to present her gift to me.

It was as though we'd stepped into that black and white film. The room exactly fashioned to mirror this one. Even down to the rope hanging from the ceiling, waiting to be secured to the back of the submissive and used to raise her high.

I'd advised Andrea she must earn that right to suspension.

As she sat at my feet she shuddered with anticipation.

"Good girl," I said. "You chose this one for me?"

"Yes, sir."

She trembled with excitement, her cheeks flushed, and her eyes wide.

I rose from the chair and gestured for her to stand and lean forward on the hand rests of the chair with her butt out and ready for her punishment.

I felt a rush of arousal at seeing her so subservient, so tranced-out - proving she was just as turned on by the way her thighs shone with dampness.

Gently tapping her first with the whip, I judged her tolerance to the pain, with each strike gauging the way she reacted, her deep-throated moan as the leather met her butt, the way she shoved her ass out for more, the way her fingers clutched the armrest and quickly relaxed again.

Moving down to her sex, I parted her labia with my left hand and holding the whip with my right, I tapped it against her clit.

She moaned. "I want to be strung up, Master."

"Soon." I continued to use the whip, the sound of the strikes echoing, my cock rock hard and feeling the rush of blood, my balls urging me to take her.

I sent her over for another accoutrement, her pretty ass wangling as she crawled back to the table. She'd know I'd see evidence of her arousal shining brightly beneath the lights, her pussy spasms of need.

We continued on with this hypnotic rhythm, her crawling on all fours, heading off to bring me another instrument of torture.

Finally, she could no longer hold off. She crawled back to me with a vibrator between her teeth.

With her now sitting in the chair with her legs splayed on either side, I leaned toward her and said, firmly, "You may regret this choice."

I ran the vibrating toy over her nipples and watched her squirm, those rippling buds rising even more, pink points firm.

"Is this what you want?" I lowered the vibrator and held it above her pubic bone.

"Lower, Master," she burst out.

I rested it on her clit and held it there. "Remember, no talking without permission." I lifted it again. "Do you understand the rules?"

She nodded furiously, her gaze moving from her sex back up to the toy.

"By bringing me this," I said, "You're asking for clit play?"

Her head fell back. "Oh, God, yes, clit play, Master." She slapped her hand over her mouth, realizing what she'd done.

"Stand."

She looked exhilarated.

"However," I said sternly. "Play is always on my terms."

I led her into the center of the room.

Within several minutes she was suspended from that central rope, her arms above her, her body almost standing, with her feet barely off the ground, thighs splayed open and bound with rope.

"Subs may never ask for pleasure," I told her. "This is against the rules. So, you will be punished." I ran my hand through her dark hair and tucked the locks behind a shoulder. "This will also serve as your education."

She leaned into me, affectionately rubbing her face against my hand.

"You did not do your homework. Want to know how I know that?"

She gave a wary nod.

"You brought over a vibrator to me. It was a test and you failed it."

Her eyes widened.

"Had you done your homework, you'd know that it is only your master who chooses your rewards...your pleasures."

Her gaze followed me.

"So, let's go over what a submissive and master relationship really is." I strode around her, arms behind my back, a professorial air to my stride. "We have two types of relationships. Firstly, there is the one where lovers live their day-to-day life with full emersion. The other, like ours, where we merely get to play this role during sex—"

"I know that." She burst out.

I spanked her hard. "You rile me up on purpose?"

"Can't help it."

"You will do as you are told."

Her irises dilated and she looked wild and exhilarated, her skin still flushed from her beating.

She hung majestically from the rope, patient and listening as I strolled around her, offering my dark monologue on what was expected of a submissive, instructing her on the many aspects of our world. Finally she swooned; surrendering with understanding.

"Is this what you expected?" I asked.

"It's more. It feels so safe." She shook her head as though trying to comprehend her feelings. "So...nurturing."

I knelt before her and nestled into her sex, running my tongue along her. She tasted incredible, her clit felt so soft and alluring it almost sent me over the edge.

She let out a long moan.

"This," I whispered, my breath warm on her clit. "Giving yourself to me proves trust. My strikes to your flesh heighten your pleasure."

"Permission to speak?"

"Granted."

"Am I allowed my toy now?"

"I have something even better," I said. "A session is always as your master dictates. He knows what is best for you."

I left her hanging there.

She moved her body wantonly, her feminine curves swaying in a shimmering show of need.

I brought over a small box and lifted the lid. From within it I brought out three small silver balls.

"Thighs wider, please." Taking my time, I inserted the Venus Balls into her vagina. She shuddered as they went in further.

"Now, where were we?" Strolling around her, tweaking her nipples, caressing her skin firmly, I gauged how far I could push her. "No coming without permission."

"Yes, Master."

I retrieved the paddle from the slew of other accoutrements and brought it over to her. I swung her forward and when she flew back I spanked her ass. With each strategically aimed strike to her butt, pleasure ricocheted into her sex, no doubt making the balls vibrate for a few seconds within her - from the way her jaw gaped as she swung wide.

Switching on the remote to those Venus balls, I delivered a low thrum inside her pussy.

Her moans echoed around us.

"I never want to leave here," she whispered.

On and on she swung while I spanked her, and she groaned and wiggled her way through the blissful sensations of burning ass cheeks and her sex thrumming.

Her body went rigid as she neared orgasm.

I stilled her by holding the rope above. "Do not come."

"I'll try."

She moaned and settled into the swing of the rope - then her head fell back and she let out a contented sigh.

I brought over an electric vibrator - an improvement on the one she'd given to me, with its oversized rounded head that could deliver four intensity levels.

With a flick I had it at the max.

I stood before her and with a firm swing I pushed her away from me and she went flying off. When she returned to my side, I lowered the vibe and rested in on her clit, letting it buzz forcefully against her. Her eyes went wide with surprise, her body shuddering, breasts shaking, her nipples hard and yearning.

She let out a long groan. "Oh, yes, yes."

I shoved her away and she spun, gravity soon bringing her back.

I pressed the vibrator to her sex again and she tilted her hips, rocking toward it, riding the rounded head against her clit, her thighs soaked now.

I let her settle there for a while.

This sweet sub frantically pressed her clit against the vibrator's head, shuddering with tranced-out bliss.

"Is that nice?" I said.

She stuttered an inaudible answer.

Again using the rope above her for leverage, I shoved her away. Andrea's eyelids lowered, her stare glazed over in sub-space - having completely surrendered to pleasure.

She was close to coming again.

Another shove and she swung wide.

"You've been a very good girl," I said.

She nodded aggressively. Her bravery for enduring this tease was so impressive I knew holding off any longer could cause her to pass out - her need was so raw, primal.

I stilled the rope and pressed the vibrator firmly against her clit, rubbing it up and down her sex. I leaned in to suckle on one of her pert nipples. She shuddered violently, her hips rocking, her sex riding the vibrator, her erotic cries filling the room.

Suspended there, I forced her through another climax.

She whimpered through the pleasure, her limbs weak and her sex seemingly sensitive from yet another orgasm.

"Mercy, sir," she burst out.

"That's not your safe word?"

"Glass, it's glass!"

I lifted the vibrator and kissed her forehead.

She looked up at me. "How is it possible?"

"How is what possible?"

"You know my body so well?"

"We're still in session."

She looked ecstatic.

I carried the vibrator back to the table. Gently, I eased out the Venus balls, too, and she squirmed at my touch.

Andrea's arousal was still at fever-pitch, her thirst unquenchable. I marveled at her stamina and how it matched mine so well.

I could do this to her all night.

Freeing her from the rope, I lifted her and carried her out of there, along the hallway and up the central staircase. We made our way along another hallway and I nudged open a door with my back, carrying Andrea inside.

A four-poster bed rested in the center of the room. The vaulted ceiling was startlingly high.

She gasped her surprise.

Twenty or so bouquets of flowers surrounded us here and there, an array of color and floral scents intermingling - roses, lilies and sunflowers. This dreamy décor leant an ethereal air to the room, one that suited Andrea's femininity.

She lifted her head to better look at me.

"I can be romantic," I said.

"Is this your way of bringing me down slowly?"

"Oh, baby," I whispered into her ear. "There's no coming down slowly with me."

In the corner, secured to the ceiling by a single chain, hung a sex swing. I carried Andrea over and she settled into it, her legs spread wide and her feet resting on the material stirrups. She eased her wrists through the straps. With a nudge I spread her thighs even wider.

She watched me undress. I threw my pants and shirt on the back of a chair.

Her gaze was drinking in my well-toned form, her focus resting on my erection. She licked her lips.

From out of the top drawer of the dresser, I ripped open the small packet and removed the toy - sliding on the vibrating cock ring.

Making my way over to her, I said, "From this angle I get to fuck you as hard as I like." I leaned in and nuzzled her neck. "Are you ready?"

Andrea gave a nod, her interest in that sex toy strapped to my hard-on causing her to blink cautiously at it.

"It's time you saw the real me, Andrea." I gripped either side of the swing and moved closer.

All that work we'd done in the hall had prepared her sex perfectly - had soaked her to perfection. My cock eased into her and I gave a shove until I was balls deep inside her, that small plastic vibe pressed against her clit and setting it ablaze with pleasure. Her head fell back, hair cascading behind her, and she let out a long moan.

"Hang on tight," I warned.

My attack was swift and sure, pummeling into her with full force. Her head and body fell back slightly so she faced the ceiling, her thighs opening and welcoming me with each strike, the swing mechanism allowing me to pull out completely and reenter her, that small buzz meeting her sex with an intense thrum.

"Come for me, sub."

She screamed through her orgasm, unable to hold back.

With a pull of the side lever we flew upward rising fifteen feet in the air and she let out another scream, wrapping her legs around my waist.

"How are you with heights?"

"You're asking me that now?" She looked down and flinched.

"Let's take your mind off it—" I leaned against her, positioning my pelvis so that the vibrator hit her sweet spot again and I rocked my cock leisurely inside her.

"Oh, that's so good." Her fingers gripped the handrails, her thighs wrapped firmly around my waist. "I'm ready."

"Sure?"

She slipped into a smile. "I've never been so ready."

The force with which I took her made us swing around fast, my hips a brilliant piston fucking her with intense precision and causing her to tremble and moan through her pleasure.

We spun around; swinging to and fro.

Andrea leaned back.

"You will come again," I demanded. "Show me. Prove your pussy is mine to command."

We came together, yelling through our climaxes.

Overcoming gravity - wild and freely fucking in midair.

This shocking pleasure forced my thoughts to scatter, my hips thrusting, slamming into her, fulfilling her need to be taken so fiercely, my warmth filling her.

Our bodies still and rigid, too gone to move, locked in raging orgasms.

Eventually, when the ability to think rationally again had returned, I lowered the seat to the ground.

We tumbled onto the large four-poster bed.

I rolled on top of her, leaning on my arms for support.

She peered up at me, her face flushed, exhilarated. "What happens now?"

"This—" Nuzzling into her neck, I kissed her affectionately, bestowing pecks and licks until she was sighing with abandon.

"Now we make love." Trailing my tongue down her chest, suckling pert nipples as I moved lower, tenderly paying special attention to her sex, all the way to her feet and sending shivers throughout her body.

I worshiped her with gentle caresses which were a stark contrast to the hours we'd left behind, proving I'd read that she needed this too, her yearning to be nurtured and loved - deserving this attention that would last the rest of the night.

By morning, the scent of flowers helped lull us to sleep. Andrea's fingernails kneaded my forearms as she drifted off, her breathing soft, sighs of completeness.

My arms wrapped around her possessively.

CHAPTER 13

"WE HAVE A PROBLEM, Mr. Booth." Dominic Geddings' tone was dour.

"I got here as fast as I could," I said, throwing my suit jacket to a waiting submissive.

She caught it and lowered herself to the ground, bowing her head. The pretty girl was new, her red hair and inked up body a remarkable display of art. Three other nervous subs stood behind her.

Guilt for even looking at her hit me like a tsunami.

What the fuck was that?

Seriously? Mia was no longer mine and sessions spent with Andrea had a time-limit on them, and yet here was I conflicted about being surrounded by newbies. It didn't help that they looked at me with awe.

I was free to take any of them under my wing.

More like under the wing of William Blake's "The Great Red Dragon," I mused darkly. The next submissive I took on was going to be as kinky as me. Well primed. Unlike these subs who looked upon me nervously.

My special brand of dominance had always made submissives quirk.

"Say hello to the master of the house," said Dominic.

Their voices of greeting echoed.

The girl at my feet was kneeling before me in pure servitude, biting her lip, her eyes wide and suggestive, needing mastering.

"Thank you." I thought it was the reasonable response.

Dominic glared at the kneeling girl and she flew up and joined the others. They all scattered from Chrysalis's foyer.

I wondered where the redhead was taking my jacket.

"It's their first time catching sight of the director," said Dominic.

"Assistant director," I corrected.

"Dr. Cole sent me a text." He raised his Smartphone to show me. "You're to handle all issues until otherwise stated."

"Still."

We headed off down the hallway.

Dominic's walk gave away his stature - a man of authority and remarkable connections. He took care of every detail for Cameron when he was at his Beverly Hills office or out of town - or, like now, fuck knows where. Not only was Dominic an intimidating presence, he served all our legal needs with the brilliance of a high-powered attorney.

Cameron paid his salary and paid him well, but Dominic also worked for me, a point that often seemed to needle Dominic. No words were exchanged to prove this, only his short, sharp, pissy attitude toward me gave it away.

He huffed along. "I've been instructed to take all orders from you."

I gave a shrug. "Still no word from Cameron?"

"He's otherwise indisposed."

We entered Cameron's office, and this vast and well-organized domain reminded me of the man who was no longer taking my calls. Tall mahogany bookshelves chock-full of medical texts, dark furniture, and that carved central desk…an intimidating space.

We'd promised each other a long time ago that a lover would never get in the way of our friendship, but that was before Mia Lauren came on the scene. A mixture of jealousy and regret swept over me.

I'd lost my best friend as well.

"This kind of problem," said Dominic, raising his brows, "can only be dealt with at the highest level."

"So Cam's not accepting your calls either?"

"A pony was caught mingling with a sub last night."

"Sex?"

"Yes."

I grinned. "I meant male or female?"

"One of each?"

"I don't see the problem."

"They need to be expelled."

"Seems a bit harsh. After all, that's what we do here. Fuck."

"You know the rules."

"Best way to break them."

He paused to punish me with a glare. "A sub can only have sex with her master. Or with his permission—"

"What does this sub's master say?"

"He's not happy."

"He's an idiot."

"How do you know?"

"He's not fulfilling his sub. Of course she'll stray. Bring the idiot to me first."

"Looks like someone's 'hangry'?" Dominic tilted his head. "Do you need a snack first?"

"Tell them not to do it again." I brushed my hands together as in job well done.

"It's in the rule book. They were briefed on the rules. They broke them. They're out."

"I'd like to talk with them first."

"Good, you can deliver the news."

"The dominant first, please."

"He's not here."

"Where is he?"

"He only visits at weekends."

I caressed my brow. "Isn't there something in the rule book about the standard of care and nurturing of submissives?"

"He's a busy man."

"Can you have Pilar bring me coffee," I said. "While I'm here I might as well read Cam's emails."

"Dr. Cole's emails?"

"That's what I said."

"Certainly. Will there be anything else?"

"No, thank you."

He headed for the door.

"Maybe you need a snack yourself," I muttered.

"What was that?" He turned and looked at me.

"Dom," I said soothingly, "I miss him too."

He looked taken aback. "I suppose it was inevitable."

"Well, you've got me. I may not be Cole, but I'm just as passion-ate about this place."

"You better not leave us too, Mr. Booth."

"I'm sure that would make your day, Dom."

He looked offended. "I'd be devastated."

"Thought you didn't like me?"

"I'll get the pony first."

With a nod I watched him go. I sat in the office chair and fired up Cameron's sleek Apple desktop, shaking off Dom's briskness. Domi-nic's jealousy had always lingered. Cameron and I were as close as brothers and this had always seemed to make Dominic uneasy. I knew he was fond of me but he'd always favored Cameron. I'd admired his loyalty, even if I was usually on the wrong end of his penchant for discipline.

Opening the browser I searched the net for a gift that might be appropriate for Andrea. I wanted to send her something to let her know I was thinking of her and that our time spent together meant something. I settled on a *Doctor Who* Tardis Police Box mug, and a few clicks later I'd arranged to have it delivered to her home. I signed the card with my initials.

Thoughts of her soothed me and I marveled at the timing of her coming into my life.

I set about answering Cameron's emails. There were the usual requests for membership, questions on up-coming functions, and a few messages from exclusive clients from overseas. An email hinted that a member of the royal family from Europe was interested in joining us. I forwarded that one onto Cameron's personal email and flagged it as priority. I scanned the others, burying myself in the drudgery of admin.

Pilar appeared in the doorway and hurried toward me carrying a tray with a silver tea urn.

I'd asked for coffee, but it was no surprise that Dominic had asked our resident housekeeper to bring me a selection of Cole Teas. The cupcake on a china plate made up for it.

Pilar seemed nervous and I made a mental run-through of our previous interaction. Usually little fazed this woman in her fifties who'd subdued her strict Catholic upbringing to serve our members - merely as our housekeeper, leaving her judgment at the door.

Without Cole here she always looked so vulnerable. Some of the doms could be hard on her, too much alpha running through their veins and without the director she probably felt his loss more than most.

"How are you?" I said.

"Good, Mr. Booth." She slid the cupcake toward me.

"Have I ever told you you'd make a great submissive?"

"Every time I see you, sir."

"It's the apron," I said. "Now that I come to think of it."

She stood tall and faced me. "I poisoned your cupcake."

I lifted the plate and sniffed it. "Great way to go, Pilar."

She tutted.

"Did you get your Christmas bonus?"

"I did, sir, thank you."

"We're doubling it."

"Why?"

"Because you deserve it."

She narrowed her gaze.

"I'm standing in for the good doctor," I said. "He'd want me to make sure you have everything you need."

"I can't accept it, sir. Dr. Cole has already spoiled me this year."

And he was also putting her kid through school. No doubt there was an underlying concern that should she lose this job, her son's future was jeopardized.

I flicked open the computer. "Pay raise instead then?"

"What will Dr. Cole say? Maybe we should wait."

"I'm the boss this week, Pilar. Can't you be like the rest of L.A. and just be ruthless for at least one day?"

She looked sympathetic. "How are you?"

"Great, you?"

"You're heart is breaking," she said. "Dr. Cole is very naughty."

"Sounds like someone's been gossiping?"

"You men think you can play games and there'll be no consequences."

"We like pain as you well know."

"You hide it well. But I know. I know you very well."

"Love you too, Pilar."

"He has a tail sticking out of him."

I arched a brow.

"Man dressed as pony. Waiting outside with Mr. Geddings."

Usually we kept the ponies hidden from Pilar. But not today, apparently.

"Well, why didn't you say? Send them both in."

She made her way around to my side of the desk, grabbed my head and planted a kiss to the top. I marveled how in a few seconds flat she could make me feel like a little boy again with her sweetness.

"Bye, Pilar." I gestured to the door.

When she reached it, she turned. "You're a good man, Mr. Booth."

I lifted the cupcake and took a bite, smiling. "Red velvet!"

"Your favorite."

"Go find me the antidote. You know I can never resist your treats." I wiggled my eyebrows.

She gave a playful frown and hurried out.

Within seconds Dominic and his six foot pony stood before me. The twenty-something perfectly bridled blond towered proud and confident, his tack binding his body. He stood beside Dominic, that phallus wedged well within his ass and its lush long tale protruding grandly. The leather-donned man held his hands behind his back, head high, his line of sight diverted above me, and nervous too, by the way he swallowed his fear.

"Thank you, Mr. Geddings," I said. "Please also bring the accused submissive."

"At the same time?" he said sharply.

"Yes, two birds and all that." I took another bite of cupcake and licked icing off my fingers.

"Certainly, sir," said Dominic frowning.

He left the room in a huff.

Chewing, and a little more casual than was needed, I rose and came round to the other side of the desk. "Come here."

The young man stepped forward.

"Explain yourself," I said.

"Please." He let out a sob, his accent pure northern British. "Don't throw me out. I promise to never so much as look at another submissive again."

"Where's the fun in that?"

He blinked his confusion. "I couldn't help myself. She's so pretty."

"How long have you known her?"

He broke my stare.

"What's your name?"

"Jason, sir." He slumped to his knees, head bowed and his body shaking.

"Last name?"

"Harris."

"Have we met before?"

"Yes, I served you a drink at the ball a few weeks ago."

"That's right." I took in his pretty face, those high cheekbones, startling green eyes, his body taut and fit from all the training we provided. His bare chest toned, his manhood tucked away behind that leather codpiece.

"Stand, please."

Tears stained his face; he'd been crying.

"Do I scare you that much?"

"Only because you have the power to let me stay."

I made my way over to the filing cabinet and within seconds I'd discreetly entered the ten digit pass code. The third drawer popped open. I fingered the alphabetic files until I reached his.

Cameron profiled each member, taking a special interest in their histories. Reading his scribbled notes I soon learned from Cameron's summary just who Jason Harris was according to his analysis. He'd been recruited from London via Arc's School of Ponies, a prestigious school in Highgate that trained well and prepared a young man with a fetish for a place like Chrysalis. If I threw Harris out the damage would be long lasting. There were few places that understood the delicate management of a psyche that obsessed with not only Pony Play, but full emersion in the lifestyle. Jason had two more months left here before being packed back off to England to return to his day job working as computer specialist. The last thing we needed was a computer hacker with a grudge.

With the file put away and the cabinet re-locked I made my way back over to him. Taking my time I repositioned his bridle, running my hands over his chest to tighten the straps of his harness, and within seconds his codpiece was off and discarded on the floor, his erection rising out of dark curls.

"Well done, Mr. Harris," I said, freeing his balls.

His cock twitched and his face flushed brightly.

"You understand your crime?" I said.

"I do, sir." He glanced down at his nakedness and swooned into subspace.

"And you understand why punishment is indicated?"

"Whatever you deem suitable."

"Good."

A knock at the door indicated our other culprit had arrived.

She entered in a flurry of short stark white hair, which on a twenty-something submissive made her look nymph-like.

It reminded me of Andrea's wig and I had to shake my head to throw out that thought.

The girl was naked, other than a red thong, her big brown eyes nervously flitting to Harris and back to me. She flung herself at my feet.

"What's your name?" I said.

"Trixie."

"Real name?" I said sternly.

"That is my real name." She rose up on her heels and gave the sweetest smile.

Leaning back on the desk with my arms folded across my chest, I put my sternest face on. "So, your master leaves and you betray his trust?"

"He was the one to put us together in the first place," said Harris. "He left for a week and we thought he might be okay with us playing together again."

"By playing you mean fucking?" I said.

Harris peered down, his face full of shame.

"Don't do it again," I said.

"So we can stay?"

Trixie gasped her relief.

"Yes, but Mr. Geddings would expect a punishment."

"Thank you, sir," said Harris.

Within minutes I'd retrieved the small saddle from Cameron's office cabinet and secured the leather riding equipment to Harris's back, the size and style of the seat created merely for human pony play; a small leather cock rising out at the base.

"Up," I ordered Trixie.

She stood before me making frequent glances over to the saddle. Gently, I eased off her thong and she parted her legs to step out of it. I threw it behind her.

"Down," I ordered Harris and gestured for Trixie to mount.

She straddled his back and slid down onto it, her soft moan of pleasure proving that small protruding leather cock was now buried deep inside her. She wiggled her hips to better enjoy it and her thighs trembled. "Thank you, sir."

I ran my hand over her head. "Is that comfortable, sweetheart?"

"Yes, thank you, sir." She leaned forward, her toes curling.

"You may come at will," I told her.

She gave a nod; cheeks flushed; she'd slipped into subspace.

I turned to her pony and said firmly, "Stand."

He rose to his feet, balancing Trixie as he leaned forward slightly taking her weight with the ease of a primed sportsman, his serious expression that of a working pony. His erection curved and rock hard.

"Circle the office," I said.

He aimed for the far corner, trotting around the far reaches of the room. Trixie's moans echoed behind him as she bobbed up and down on his back, her head resting against him, her expression full of wonder - with every jerk forward that leather cock thrusting deeper.

I returned to the office chair and threw my legs onto the desk, grabbed the mouse to shake the browser awake and continued answering emails.

And finished off my cupcake.

CHAPTER 14

DOMINIC'S INTRIGUED STARE stayed on Harris as he looped around us again, Trixie's moans proving she was cantering through her third orgasm.

"Well, if expulsion is off the table," said Dominic, kneeling to retrieve Trixie's thong. "A punishment might be indicated?" He gestured to the galloping pair. "Instead of this?"

I pushed my chair back from the desk. "*This* is their punishment, Dom."

"They seem to be enjoying it."

Harris's face was flushed with excursion, his cock harder than ever, a shiny bead of pre-cum on the tip, his ride squealing through another climax.

Arching my fingers together I studied them as they came back into view.

"So they're staying, I assume?" said Dominic loud enough for them to hear.

"They are."

"I'll have Trixie's master call you."

"I appreciate that," I said. "He needs to add an addendum in his contract with Trixie that states she's allowed to play if he goes away for more than four days. Understand?"

Trixie's scream of pleasure made Dominic flinch. "Here, please."

They came to a stop, both breathless and wearing contented smiles.

"You're so merciful," I mouthed to Dominic. "I'd planned on another hour."

He waved to them. "Time to be bathed and fed." Dominic opened the door and gestured towards the hallway.

Harris cantered out with Trixie bobbing up and down on his back, her face full of happiness, her arms wrapped around his neck.

The door closed behind them.

I pulled out my phone and went to text Cameron, ready to tell him what a complete bastard he was for ignoring my calls.

His number lit up my phone and I punched the screen. "Heard you're bailing on my party?"

"I'm sorry." Cameron sounded tired.

"I left you a message at your office to call me. Thought you'd lost your phone."

"I'm in New York."

The news jolted me and I sat up. "Manhattan?"

"Yes."

This was unlike him. We usually knew each other's moves. I buried my unease. "I wanted to give you the heads up about your Cole Teas shares. Though I'm assuming your dad might have mentioned it by now."

"Richard."

"Hey, are you okay?"

"Hostile takeover. Hasn't hit the press."

A wave of nausea hit me. "Fuck."

The line went quiet.

I now felt like a selfish ass for hating him for going radio silent. "Talk to me," I coaxed, unnerved at being this far away.

"I'm here to salvage."

"How's your dad?"

"Not good."

I tried to find the right words to comfort him, but all I could say was, "You don't have too much invested in Cole shares compared to the other stock, so you're solid financially."

"Why is that?"

"I manage your shares." I sounded like an asshole. "Can I do anything?"

"You've always loved sharks, Richard. I never asked why?"

Typical Cameron, following an intuitive lead which at face value always seemed so disassociated with the subject. His brilliant mind a million leaps ahead of the rest of us.

"You did ask me once, during a session," I said.

"That's right."

"I told you to fuck off and stop asking me questions."

"I remember."

"Hadn't talked for weeks. You cracked me open like a nut. Used a psychological sledgehammer on me. Now you can't get me to shut up." I gave a sigh. "Sharks keep the ecosystem in balance."

"You're searching for balance."

"I suppose we all are. You know me. If it's frightening I have to find out why. Sharks are not unlike humans in that if you show you're not intimidated they'll leave you alone. Stare them off. Bully them back and they relent." The madness of it made me laugh.

"What's so funny?"

"You were feared at Harvard. You intimidated everyone with your intellect. The girls were too scared to approach you and the men weren't quite sure how to take you."

"I was friendly."

"Your quick wit could decimate an ego," I told him. "When we first met, I was immediately intrigued."

"Are you saying I'm like a shark?"

"You're misunderstood."

"You always got me."

"Same here," I said. "Want me to fly out there?"

"I've got this, Richard. This feels like self-fulfilling prophecy."

"Get your shark fin on."

He always led me to the clues of the subconscious and my own revelation found me in this mist of my thoughts: there was only one way Andrea could overcome her fear.

And she'd entrusted me to be her guide through this valley.

Cameron, too, was entering uncharted territory but if anyone could rise above the fray, thrive under this kind of pressure, he could. But he'd have to be willing to surrender first and Cameron was always in control. Always.

"Prepare to freefall," I whispered.

He let out a slow, steady breath.

"Cameron," I kept my voice low, "sharks can see in the dark."

Having comforted him, or hoping I had, I sat back and stared at the screen.

More emails were flooding into his inbox, strangers reaching out to the club's director. Most of them would never get to see the inside of this place.

Knowing Cameron was going through such pain made my gut tighten. He has Mia with him, I reassured myself, though now more than ever their love would be tested.

My thoughts drifted to my current client, our next session imminent. This particular subject required a firm handling. Andrea Buckingham needed a submersion unlike any other.

I lifted the phone and waited for Professor Isaac Loftin to pick up.

He answered, using his usual intense tone.

"I'm going to pay you a visit," I told him. "I'm bringing a friend. Prepare the cage."

CHAPTER 15

SAN ONOFRE HAD no idea it was winter; the morning sun beat down on us in a blast of heat, the breeze welcoming at seven in the morning.

I loved having Andrea all to myself. We sat on the end of the pier and ate Bagels and Lox from the picnic she'd prepared and sipped our coffee we'd bought along the way.

To any witnesses we were two lovers lost in thought, merely enjoying each other's company. It was easy to just be with her.

We'd known each other just over a week now, yet it felt like we'd always been friends. As though she had always been waiting for me; Andrea had become a bright prelude to the rest of my life.

Within the hour we'd made our way along the pier and found our tethered speed boat.

The Monterey swept us fast over the water and we soon left the wharf behind us.

With a thrust of the engine, I opened the throttle and it carried us out farther onto the sprawling blue ocean. We settled into this exhilarating rhythm. Andrea could escape completely out here, both of us leaving our troubles on land.

She pressed her hand down on the top of her hat to prevent it from flying off, and peered over her big sunglasses. "This is fun! What a great idea."

I beamed at her.

Ocean spray covered us and she let out a laugh. "I haven't been on this kind of adventure in forever."

"We're going somewhere very special, Andrea."

She squealed with happiness - the thrilling view of the vast blue ocean before us, waves lapping.

After twenty minutes of navigating by way of the GPS the *Score Settled* appeared on the horizon, a sixty-foot catamaran looming in sight.

With a thrust I directed us closer and closed the gap.

After carefully aligning alongside her I killed the engine and the water buffered us flush against the catamaran.

"We're changing boats?" she asked.

"For a while," I said. "Visiting old friends."

We threw a wave above us to the three smiling crew members who leaned over to greet us. After securing our boat to theirs, I assisted Andrea up the rear steps and we boarded.

Introductions were made and she shook hands with our skipper, Isaac Loftin, professor of oceanography and his coworker, Todd Mayweather. Their research assistant was twenty-two year old Rachel McNeil. Their sun-kissed smiling faces proved they were right where they wanted to be. As expected, they were unfazed by having a celebrity aboard and went out of their way to make Andrea feel welcome.

"It's been too long," said Isaac, patting my back.

"I agree," I said. "Work's gotten in the way. I've missed this. How have you been, Isaac?"

"Never better. You?"

"Just wonderful," I said. "I'm excited to be here."

He turned to Andrea. "We have a great new satellite tracking system installed thanks to this man."

"You'd have gotten funding for it eventually," I said.

"Grants take too long to get approved," he said. "Wanna take a look?"

"We'd love to." I led Andrea to the bridge, and we stepped down into the high-tech control room. We peered out onto the front deck through the sweeping wide window and admired the new dashboard with its state-of-the-art sonar system along with the satellite tracking hardware. All housed in luxury wood trim.

"Are we going scuba diving?" asked Andrea.

"We are."

Her face lit up. "Are there dolphins?"

"Sometimes."

She glanced at the console. "Can you see them on the radar?"

"Yes, if they're around."

"What's that?" She neared the sonar and pressed a fingertip to the screen following the blip.

Isaac appeared in the doorway. "Suits are prepped and tanks checked."

"Thank you, Isaac," I said. "We'll go get changed."

With Andrea's hand in mine, I led her off the bridge and we descended into the lower deck.

I opened the door and gestured for Andrea to go first. She gasped when she realized she was standing on a clear glass floor. Beneath our feet was a full view of the ocean's underwater flora, fauna, and reefs. The reflection threw a shimmering light over her face as she dared to move in farther, her dark hair glinting with highlights.

Her expression was pure delight. "I'm scared to walk on it."

"It's extremely sturdy." I arched a brow. "Obviously."

To our left was an entire wall of glass, ocean life swimming by.

"I'd be happy to just stay in here," she said.

"Then you'll miss all the fun." I closed the door. "Take off your clothes."

She placed her tongue between her teeth and bit it playfully.

"Later," I said.

We undressed and Andrea was wearing her bikini just as I'd told her too. We took our time shimmying in to our diving suites. I helped her zip hers up.

Andrea lifted one of the two Neptune Space G masks and examined the sleek design. "This is nice. Looks high-tech."

"It is."

The full face mask looked more like something a fighter pilot might wear, with its streamlined visor and molded silicon rubber to fit snuggly over the face.

I took it from her and turned it over to show her. "See this? We can talk to each other while we're down there and communicate with Isaac, too."

"I love that!"

I drew closer to her. "I suppose now's the right time to ask."

"Ask what?"

"Are you menstruating?"

She flashed a smile. "Oh no, is this some kind of kinky activity?"

"You mean fucking under water?"

She blushed. "Yes."

"No."

"Why would you ask me—" Her eyes dropped to the glass floor. "No, I'm not. Richard? Tell me there aren't sharks down there."

"Welcome aboard the UCLA official shark research lab. Here they track, tag, and monitor the great white shark."

She glanced down at her wetsuit.

"We'll be in a cage, Andrea."

"Hell no."

"That blip you saw. Her name's Pearl. She's only twelve feet."

"Pearl?" Andrea stared down and her eyes swept the water.

"All we have to do is sit tight, chum, and wait."

She swallowed hard. "You want me to get in a cage?"

"Actually, it's glass. Better view."

"Don't need a great view." She looked pale. "Won't it be hard to tell...?"

"Yes, it will seem as though we're right in front of her."

"Sounds dangerous."

"No more than crossing the street."

"I don't believe you."

"Come on," I said. "Let's go have some fun."

With a firm grip on Andrea's arm, I led her up to the bow where Isaac and Todd were waiting for us. Isaac helped Andrea with her mask and secured her oxygen tank to her back, and slid the weights into her belt. Todd helped me with mine.

After a minute of breathing through the mask again it felt natural and I admired the 360 degree view of the wide visor. I moved slower now, the weights strapped around my waist compromising my movement, the slight restriction of the suit.

Within ten minutes we were good to go.

"Checking the comms," I said. "Andrea, how's that for you?"

"I can hear you," she said, peering through her visor.

Isaac turned toward the bridge where he received a thumbs up from Rachel who was screening the sonar. "Comms loud and clear for us, too," he said.

Andrea froze. "Richard, I can't."

I signaled for Rachel to turn off the sound so we could talk in private.

Taking Andrea's hands in mine I stared into her eyes. "Fear is nothing more than an illusion. It doesn't exist."

"What I'm feeling is real."

"Thoughts are not reality."

She mulled over my words. "How can this possibly help me?"

"The answer lies down there." I pointed to the water. "It's waiting for you."

"What if that shark kills me?"

"Face her and you can face anything."

She grazed her teeth over her lower lip. "I don't see the connection."

"Because you're blinded by fear."

"Fuck you for doing this. Fuck you for not warning me."

"You wouldn't have come."

"It doesn't seem right."

"This is what it means to be alive."

"I should never have asked you to help me. You have no idea what you're doing."

"I've swum with sharks so many times I've lost count. I know them well."

"I'm not insured for stuff like this."

"Take a breath."

She gave an unconvincing nod.

"You knew I could help you," I said. "Trust it. Trust me."

"Okay." She shook her head.

I signaled to Rachel to turn the comms back on. "I'll go first."

"She's a beauty," said Isaac. "You're one lucky lady."

"You are all completely mad," she said.

The top of the glass cage bobbed above the surface. I sat on the edge of the boat and tugged on my fins.

Andrea sat beside me and tugged on hers. "I'm not going in."

"I know." I beamed at her.

"Can sharks tell if you're scared?"

"No." I threw a glance at Isaac.

We both knew that should we cower down there, turn our backs on Pearl, or appear distressed, the shark would know. She'd evolved to detect animals in distress.

"I can do this." Andrea's breathy voice echoed in my earpiece.

"Yes, you can" I said. "Ready?"

She gave a nod.

I swung my legs over the edge, placed my hands on both sides of the cage and lowered myself down into it. The water was warm and welcoming and those weights felt lighter now, an easy swell around me. Turning, I raised my hands to Andrea and she gave a final nod of consent as she too used the glass side for leverage.

She lowered into my arms, her gaze catching the two large black floatation devices, the buoys needed to keep us afloat.

From above, Isaac worked the hydraulics and we were jolted out.

"We'll check our equipment and then we'll continue," I told Andrea.

"Sounds good." She gripped my forearm.

Beneath the surface we stared into each other's eyes, both of us testing whether or not our masks were leak proof and our oxygen tanks were delivering the right amount of air.

"You've done this before," I said. "You're a natural."

"Yes, but that was on vacation. Haven't dived in years."

"No ascending with your lungs full," I warned.

"I remember."

"So we're good to go?"

"We're good to go," she said.

"Going down," Isaac's confident voice streamed in.

We descended slowly, staring at each other, doing a cautious final check to make sure there were no leaks in our masks. Buffered by the water, we could hear the sound of our own breathing.

Isaac's voice came across, reassuring us that all checks up there were in order.

"Breathe normally," I said.

"This is normal," she said. "I always breathe like this when I'm shark bait."

I chuckled. "This will be easier than facing those sharks back in Hollywood."

"I want to believe you." She gripped me. "Promise me this cage is built to withstand an attack? Perhaps I should have asked that before getting in?"

"It's solid."

"What if I pee?" Andrea burst out laughing. "Will the shark go for me?"

"The safest place is underwater. As long as we don't look like wounded seals." I gave her a sideways glance. She didn't need to know that sharks would be curious once they caught sight of us.

A passing visual sweep revealed only a couple of yellowtail's gliding by. Isaac would see Pearl first on the sonar, but we'd already decided not to tell Andrea when she was approaching, wanting to give her the chance to view the shark in the distance swimming majestically toward us.

We heard a splash above and the water became tinged red with blood. A dead fish head bobbed around.

"Chum," I said. "We're hailing our beauty."

"How is this meant to help me?" whispered Andrea.

I turned her around to face the front of the glass and then slid in front of her, protecting her body with mine. She wrapped her arms around my chest and hugged me.

The water was calm, relaxing, and it felt easy to leave the world behind. The only sound was that of our breathing, the sensation of Andrea tight and trembling against my back.

"Do you come here often?" She giggled.

"As much as I can."

Isaac's voice sounded clear in my earpiece. "Your man here funds the boat, Andrea."

"It's one of the many charities our company oversees," I said.

"And we're eternally grateful," said Isaac.

"I'm grateful for the work you do," I said. "It's changing the way people see sharks and enlightening them to how important they are. I've been away too long."

"Don't let that happen again," said Isaac. "You know we love having you here."

"Me too," I said. "This is good work you're doing. Sharks are vital to keep the ecosystem in order, Andrea. Without them this finely balanced structure will collapse."

Isaac piped in, "Sharks have survived over 450 million years, and many species are threatened with extinction."

"Here she is," I said soothingly.

Out of the gloomy depths rose that familiar glide, all twelve feet of her, both old and new scars running down the side of her neck and that tag in her fin still secure.

"Pearl," I said softly.

Andrea's grip tightened. "Oh, my God."

"Nice and calm."

"It's too big."

The large grey shark loomed close, making a passing sweep, dark eyes surveying us as its nose nudged a piece of fish away. She whipped around fast, jaw gaping, serrated teeth up against the glass, and she turned again sharply, shying away, cautious, moving through the water with a flip of her long tale.

"She's injured," whispered Andrea.

"You mean the scars on her gills?" I said.

"Yes, look, she's been attacked."

"What you're seeing is very natural," I said. "Those are sustained during sex. They're from where her mate bit onto her to hold her still."

"Really?"

"Yes."

"Looks painful."

"It heals."

Andrea pressed her fingertips into my ribs; perhaps a silent hint at her surprise at the roughness of the species.

"See how brave she is?" I said.

"She doesn't seem to have an issue with being brave."

Pearl pulled back away from us, reacting to something unseen, and dived, disappearing into the murky depths.

"Oh, thank God," said Andrea.

A jolt of adrenaline surged through my veins. "How far away?" I asked Isaac.

"She's at nine o'clock," he replied.

"I see her."

The shark was at least eighteen feet long and there was no surprise that she'd threatened Pearl and caused her to swim away, with her grey and white body mass startlingly big - a gigantic heart-stopping sea creature.

My gust twisted in knots as she approached. A wave of exhilaration flooded over me.

This number one predator made a sweep around our cage, her eyes on us; large gills rippling, enormous tale flicking.

Andrea was silent.

"You okay back there?"

"No."

The shark circled, her two thousand pounds threatening to crush the cage should she swing her body around violently toward us. Her prowling proved she was hunting.

God, she was spectacular. A breathtaking wonder.

Andrea's chin rested on my shoulder and I sensed she'd surrendered, fighting was useless, our vulnerability startling.

"Her name's Joy," I whispered.

"Lovely."

"Isn't she gorgeous?"

"I'd bite you if I didn't have this thing on."

Isaac's chuckle came from my earpiece.

The shark's jaw gape exposed row upon row of triangular serrated teeth, a mouth that could swallow a man whole; she gnawed the corner of the glass causing us to rock.

She flipped away and circled the cage. Water buffered us.

With a powerful lunge she struck out - her teeth embedded in one of the two floats above and it became nothing but hissing punctured material in her mouth as she shook it.

Our refuge rocked to and fro as we were jolted about.

"Richard!" Andrea snapped.

"We're fine," I said. "As long as she doesn't—"

As though in slow motion we watched Joy flip her tale and explore above us. That floating bloody chum was too close to the second float. She caught that black rubber buoy between her serrated teeth.

And crushed it.

I spun around and hugged Andrea into me. "Hang on. I've got you."

From within our glass cage we descended into the murky depths.

CHAPTER 16

THE SWIRL OF the ocean enveloped us during our slow fall, bubbles surrounding us as the cage rocked.

My ears were popping from the pressure.

Andrea's frantic breathing filled my earpiece.

"Andrea," I said firmly. "Do exactly as I say, understand?"

"Yes," she burst out, her body crushed against mine, her arms flailing.

"Focus and trust me." I brought her arms to her sides. "I need you to stay still."

I didn't want her to look like a seal.

"Oh, my God," she said.

"Stay calm."

She gripped my forearms. "Yes."

Our fall slowed even more and I stared up to see that the chain above us remained secure.

Isaac's voice sounded eerily quiet. "Are you both okay?" Any injuries?"

"We're fine."

Andrea's eyes were filled with terror.

A jolt let us know we'd stopped falling.

I took a quick glance around us. "See, told you it'd be fun."

Adrenaline set my veins alight, my focus fusing together time and space, calculating; those well-practiced drills kicking in.

"Richard, what are we going to do?"

I pressed my mask against Andrea's and stared into her deep brown eyes. "I've got this. We'll be on the surface in no time."

"Really?"

"Sure. Look down."

"Will I see a shark?"

"Our way out."

She tilted her head and blinked into the murkiness. A few feet below us sat another cage, its metal bars sturdy.

"We're going to switch cages?" she said.

"Yes," I said. "It's a walk in the park. Isaac, can you lower us any further?"

"That's as far as I can get you," he said. "We're working on the hydraulics of the metal cage."

"What's holding us up?"

"Technical hitch," he said. "We're working on it."

"See," I reassured her. "This is just like any other day. Like shopping at the mall during the sales."

"I have a personal shopper," she said, scanning the water around us. "Will Joy come back for us? We're like two wounded seals. I heard sharks love seals."

"So how does that work?"

"What?"

"A personal shopper?"

She flashed an annoyed glance my way. "Sounds so stupid now. Can you pull us up, Isaac?"

"Look at me," I said. "The floats are gone. We can't ascend. We have to move to the other cage."

"It's too far away."

"Can you bring the other cage up closer?" I asked Isaac.

"We're leaking hydraulic fluid," he said. "But we've found the source and should have it fixed in no time."

I glanced at the bar on Andrea's oxygen tank. She had fifteen minutes left. "Andrea, I need you to breathe slower."

"Why?"

"I don't suck air like you." I arched an amused brow. "Actually, no one sucks quite like you."

She thumped my arm and I burst out laughing.

"I promise I'll take care of you." I smiled. "I'll have us up on that boat in no time."

Her lips trembled. "Hurry up."

"We're on it."

The cage below jolted and shifted slightly.

"We need you to be our eyes," said Isaac.

"Will do," I said. "Keep it coming. It's ten feet away."

The metal cage neared, rising out of the deep toward us and I counted down for Isaac until it was as close as it could go.

"Richard." Andrea pointed.

Three sharks circled below. Those smaller sharks were our warning sign. If they scattered, Joy could be close.

"Can you bring it any closer?" I said. "There's still a gap."

"That's as close as we can get it," said Isaac, "otherwise the wires might get caught in your cage. That would not be good."

"What would happen then?" Andrea asked.

We'd be stuck down here forever.

"I'd have to untangle it," I said.

"What happens if one of those sharks comes close when we're transferring?" she asked, her voice sounding panicked.

"I can handle them," I said. "Now listen, I'm going to unclip the bottom of the glass. As soon as I do it you drop and swim to the other cage."

"Completely exposed?"

"I'll handle the sharks. You concentrate on getting to that cage."

There was no time to lose focus. No time for regret.

I gripped Andrea's forearms and held her as still as possible, buffered slightly by the swell. "So, this is the plan. I check for sharks. When I don't see any I unlatch the base. You swim straight to the cage."

"And you're right behind me?"

"I'll be right beside you."

"Then we get hoisted up?"

"Yeah, see? It'll be easy."

"Looking good on the sonar," Isaac piped in. "The point's at thirty feet."

And by point he meant Joy.

"Okay, I'll count to five. You face downward ready to go," I said. "Isaac, the move is imminent."

"We've got you," he said.

Staring into Andrea's visor, I checked for signs to see if she was ready and if this was something she thought she was capable of. A discreet glance at the back of her tank showed oxygen was down to twelve minutes.

"Wait," she said. "Let's talk it through again."

"Sure."

"How long will it take to swim to the second cage?"

"Seconds."

"I don't like it."

"Yes, but looking back you will."

"We can do this, right?"

"Like I said - easy."

"How can you be so calm?"

"I know sharks."

"Will they come for us?"

"They're curious, nothing more."

A blip in my ear from Isaac. "Can we do this now, please?"

He'd no doubt caught the reading on Andrea's tank.

Or possibly caught Joy closing in.

"We're good to go," I told him.

"Wait." Andrea grabbed my arm again. "There's a shark."

I turned to see Pearl gliding by, her tale sweeping close and I waited for her to disappear into the murky distance.

"Here we go," I said, flipping over in what felt like slow motion to face downward.

Andrea followed, throwing me a wary smile.

"That's my girl," I said. "I'll talk you through it."

A few sharks lingered below to the left of the cage. From her vantage point Andrea couldn't see them.

I beamed back at her and then turned my attention to the catch. My fingers slipped off the metal clip. I went for it again.

"Something wrong?" said Andrea.

"Little stiff." I grabbed it with both hands and pulled hard, the resistance slowing me down.

Isaac's voice came over my earpiece. "Snap the others."

"And then kick the bottom out?" I said. "Good idea."

But it was the sudden movement I wanted to avoid.

"Look," said Andrea.

Following her gaze I saw the sharks swimming close by.

"See." I said. "There they go."

They disappeared into the murkiness.

The ocean swirled around us; buffering.

I wrestled with the catch and it gave. The other three went more easily, and with a nudge the glass fell away.

Leaving us more vulnerable than before.

I gave a thumbs up. "Let's move."

Andrea gestured that she was ready.

"We're moving now, Isaac," I said.

"See you soon," he said.

Propelling ourselves forward we kicked off from the cage and swam downward toward our metal sanctuary.

I held back, making sure Andrea swum into the cage first, her elegant glide hiding the fact she was probably full of terror.

She turned and gave me the thumbs up, gesturing for me to hurry, her face flushed.

Turning, my legs sinking into the cage, I raised my head to catch the lone shark as it swam above me.

Reaching out, I trailed my fingertips along her fin.

CHAPTER 17

OUR CAGE ROSE out of the depths with the skill needed to balance our safe ascent.

Andrea followed my command to exhale all oxygen from her lungs, hugging me as we rose. Those bubbles rising from her airway proved she'd obeyed.

We were greeted with more hugs on the surface.

A pat on my back from Isaac, his laughter revealing he'd found this just as exhilarating as I had. Andrea claimed she was fine, but her frantic carotid pulse proved otherwise.

Within minutes we'd returned to our cabin to change.

She was shaking, the adrenaline still racing through her body, her eyes wide as she scanned the glass bottom.

"It's one way," I said. "We're oblique to all ocean life."

She ignored me and unzipped her wetsuit.

I stepped out of mine. "I don't know about you but I'm aroused."

That gorgeous face was marred with confusion, damp flushed skin; a slight tremble.

I stood there, calm, waiting, ready for her to spill. "At no time were we in danger."

She moved closer and slapped my face hard.

"You're going to have to help me out here?" I said. "I have no idea why you're pissed off."

Her clenched fists relaxed, her eyes wild with excitement as she sprang at me, cupping her hands on either side of my face and pressing her lips to mine. We kissed passionately, our damp bodies molded together, our tongues teasing, punishing, relishing that taste of salt.

She pulled back and slapped me again.

My cock responded with a pulse of pleasure and I caught her glancing down at it.

"Andrea, you're going to kiss me again. Only this time you'll be a good girl and surrender in my arms. Understand?"

"Why should I?"

"Because now you have fire in your eyes. And I'm the one who put it there."

Her gaze fell to my lips. "You're out of your mind."

"You outdid yourself down there."

She threw an angry glance my way. "That was the most terrifying thing I've ever faced."

"Andrea, come here, now."

"No,"

"Andrea."

"We could have died down there."

"The Buddhists believe that in order to truly live we have to know what it is to die."

She let out a sob and fell into my arms, her lips on mine, giving in as I tipped her head back and owned her mouth, my tongue fucking hers as her body relaxed, relenting.

I righted her and we hugged, our bodies damp, our flesh warm, hearing the quiet creaking of the boat as it rocked beneath our feet.

I kissed her forehead. "You're reborn."

She sucked in a deep breath and pushed away from me, her stare finding the glass wall. She walked over and rested her palms against it, gazing out into the blue-green depths.

I approached and stood behind her. "Andrea?"

"I don't understand."

I bowed my head; questioning my methods.

She spun round and raised her chin defiantly. "It's gone. My fear. It's no longer—" She pressed her palm to her chest as though testing it.

From behind her a Marlin swam past. Andrea noticed the beautiful fish swim by, and she burst into laughter.

"You surrendered."

"I went beyond fear."

"What do you need, Andrea? I'll give you anything. Do anything for you. You know that."

"I need you to fuck me, Richard - just fuck me hard, okay?"

I reached round and grabbed a lock of wet matted hair at her scalp and drew her toward me, my lips firm on hers, forcing her mouth wide.

She surrendered against me.

114

Softening my kiss, our mouths explored tenderly, words no longer needed to prove we both felt her breakthrough. Her tongue danced with mine, and I heard her sob of relief as she bit my lower lip.

I lifted her, pressing her body against the glass. She wrapped her legs around my waist, my cock pressing at her entrance. A small shift and I thrust easily inside her tautness, slamming her against the window.

Our movement in perfect unison, we fell into a natural rhythm, her smiling in between a change of position. Taking her from behind now, she leaned over with her hands splayed on the glass, her butt pushed out for me, my balls striking her sex. Her groans silenced as I slapped my hand over her mouth. We went from me kneeling between her legs and worshiping her sex with my tongue, to her bowed before me, her mouth taking my cock in long firm sucks and almost making me lose control.

We settled on the glass floor, wrapped in each other's arms, rolling from one end of our small cabin to the other.

Our breathy sighs and the slapping of our bodies together the only noise we heard.

Buried deep inside her, my chest raised on my elbows while using my pelvic thrusts to take her closer, I pummeled into her, her pussy milking me, her fingernails digging deep into my back and scratching along my spine.

She was wild, and free, and tempestuous in my arms.

I loved her freckled face, those big brown eyes that looked up at me in awe, her femininity as she glided elegantly beneath me, her enduring strength.

We were a perfect balance between domination and submission, the level I'd needed but never realized - her spirit in perfect accord with mine.

She led our lovemaking and I let her. She needed to find her own way back to her own power.

Until she needed me to take over again; master her.

With her face down, her ass high in the air, I rode her from behind. There were fine fresh scratches along the left side of her neck and I ran my fingertips along them, her tender skin a victim of our fierce lovemaking.

Instinctively we froze.

Andrea's breath caught as a large shape swam directly under us. Her hands splayed out wide as though wanting to touch that great white shark. Joy swept along and yet again we were reminded of her profound size and strength.

With a flick of her enormous tale she dove into the deep.

I flipped Andrea over and stared into her eyes, seeing her look of wonder, her jaw gaping, her eyes wide.

We began laughing as we stared at each other, astounded with this moment.

I took her again, burying deep inside her as she arched her back, her dark locks spilling on the glass. Leaning low I sucked on her breasts, taking one nipple and then the other, my cock gliding in and out slowly, leisurely, savoring her.

Andrea came, moaning her pleasure.

Both of us finding our release; shuddering together.

We lay in each other's arms on the glass bottom. Safe, nurtured, with post-adrenaline exhaustion dragging us down.

Easing away, I bent to lift her, carrying her over to the small bed. We tumbled onto it, rolling into a hug. She lay atop me, her right leg thrown over my body, her arms wrapped around me.

"Talk to me," I whispered.

She let out a long, thoughtful sigh. "I've always been so coddled…protected. Never allowed to be in harm's way."

"You never got to test your boundaries."

She rested her head against my chest. "I'm still shaking."

"You're welcome."

She smiled against my neck. "I hate you."

"No you don't."

"I can't believe we just did that."

"I've tried a lot of daredevil stunts and this one tops them all." I winked at her. "It's my fave."

"You've swum with sharks before?"

"Of course."

"Maybe I'll come with you on your next adventure?"

"Bit clingy." I tickled her ribs.

She giggled and raised her head to look at me. "I'm not falling for you. If that's what you're afraid of."

"You just told me you hate me."

"To be honest, I've never seen anything quite that big."

"Why thank you, Andrea."

She thumped my arm. "The shark, I meant the shark."

"So did I!" I caught her hand and brought it to my lips, kissing her wrist.

She let out a deep sigh. "I don't want this to end."

"We can stay here for as long as we want."

She lifted her head to look at me. "I meant us."

"Confession time."

She peered up at me.

I kissed her nose. "What you experienced was a training exercise. We were never in danger. We always have a second cage. The skill is knowing when to transfer to the other one. I was in control the entire time."

She lay her head back down, her breathing lighter, her body relaxed. "I'm too tired to be angry."

"Andrea," I whispered. "Another confession." I lifted my head to see she'd fallen asleep. "I feel the same way about you."

Her eyelids fluttered and I felt the soft curl of her fingers on my chest.

CHAPTER 18

PAYBACK WAS A bitch.

I was sitting in the back of a limo wearing a ridiculous grin, having been summoned by Andrea Buckingham. She'd ordered me to drop everything and accept her invitation to "God knows where."

For a surprise I was sure to like.

She'd called just after lunch to tell me to get in the limo parked outside. Most of my work at Enthrall had been taken care of and Scarlet hadn't let me refuse this adventure, promising to handle any late afternoon calls.

We hit 4 P.M. traffic as we rolled into Ventura and I took in the new stores, restaurants, and businesses that had sprung up since I'd last visited this bustling town.

Of all the sessions I'd conducted, Andrea's would stay with me for a very long time. In fact, my thoughts often returned to our recent conversations, our many texts, and I'd even questioned whether having any more vanilla sex was advisable.

Perhaps after her training I'd leave town. That sat well with me. Once I'd delivered all she needed and it was over.

Don't think of that now. Enjoy her.

Andrea was willing to stand right along beside me and experiment with whatever I had to show her. She'd experienced a real breakthrough back on the boat, and that in itself proved we were drawing to a close.

The car pulled up at the curb.

At the top of those steps sat a large, tall fountain.

The driver leaned back to hand me a long black box. The Lux Spa was embossed on it.

Out of the car now, I took two steps at a time and made my way past the fountain and through the small mall, passing the Cheesecake Factory, and recalling that Mia had been a waitress in this very restaurant back before she'd ever known about Enthrall. She'd worked two jobs before being hired as Enthrall's secretary, the other at Willems's Art Store in Studio City.

I'd not thought about Mia for a while. Those pangs of loss had faded and it made me question what kind of relationship we'd had if it was this easy to let her go, or more startling still, what kind of friendship I now had with Andrea.

I checked in at The Lux Spa and was greeted by young female staff with fresh-faced smiles and perky personalities. Despite wanting to ask if Andrea was here, I knew I couldn't. After all, she always went by a pseudonym when out in public.

Inside the dimly lit sanctuary, I took advantage of all the amenities. I shaved and showered, spent some time in the sauna and moved on to the small pool, marveling at how long it had been since I'd pampered myself like this.

If this was Andrea's way of saying thank you, it was pretty damn fantastic, even if my heart objected to the imminent ending of us.

A staff member summoned me for my first treatment, which was to be a Sugar Shower Scrub, she informed me. I gave a smile and a shrug, having no idea what that was, my thoughts running ahead at the idea of that deep tissue massage which was apparently next.

Standing on the steps of the small, dark room, I took in the view.

A large bed in the center was strewn with damp burgundy towels and suspended high above it were an array of fine metal tubes running horizontally across.

"Exfoliating body scrub," said the middle-aged massage therapist, who advised me she'd step out for a few seconds and that I should strip off my towel and lay face down.

Curious, and willing to try pretty much anything, I whipped my towel off and lay face down on the firm bed, my face peering through the padded triangular headrest.

Soft melodic music filled the room with its soothing rhythm.

I heard a door open.

The therapist returned, and steam filling the room - only just bearable. More startling still, I was being pummeled with sprays of water from every angle.

The therapist asked if I was okay and I lied that I was.

This, this was retribution for the underwater adventure I'd put Andrea through.

Hot thick liquid poured over my legs as the masseuse's strong hands kneaded the warm sugar and water against my limbs. It scratched slightly, but felt wonderful, and the vanilla and rosemary scents were invigorating.

Fifteen minutes passed and I wondered why I'd never tried this before.

On my back now, the blindfold covering my eyes and the towel strategically placed, I endured the fall of fine water that barely missed my mouth.

Andrea really did have a sense of humor.

Surrounded by stillness, I mused whether to slip into a nap or if more pummeling from the masseuse was imminent.

The door opened and I heard the click of the lock.

Lifting my mask to see, I made out the blur of a woman at the end of the table - a stunning brunette dressed in a long red dress.

"Andrea?" I sat up.

She kicked off her heels.

Andrea moved over to the wall panel and flipped a switch. More warm water sprayed from those overhead tubes; a fountain bursting upon me.

"Well, this is a nice surprise," I said, wiping droplets from my eyes.

"Shush." She climbed onto the end of the table still dressed, her hands resting on my feet, her fingers rubbing sugar across my shins and moving up to my thighs, and higher still to reach my abdomen. "No talking."

Her dress was drenched, showing off her curves and pointed nipples, her dark locks soaked, strands dropping over her face. With her hand sliding lower across my abdomen, teasingly close to my erection, it was easy to relax into the mood and let my thoughts scatter. My limbs were taut with the tension of needing to spring up and grab her - my mind spinning with the way this beauty knew my body.

She knew I'd needed this.

Her lips wrapped around my cock. "Mmmm." She licked the tip. "You taste delicious."

My hands gripped either side of the table, my head falling back, my jaw dropping as those sensations swept over me.

What with Andrea's mouth and those fine tingles of water pressure striking each and every point of my body, I ascended into nirvana.

I lifted my head to watch the way she mastered my rock hard cock, drinking in the stunning beauty who suckled my balls, her hands running up and down the full length of me.

Pre-cum was being suckled out of me.

I reached out for Andrea, grabbing a fist full of hair and lifting her off me, sitting up, pulling her close to straddle me. She placed her thighs on either side of mine. With her hands gripping the bars above and using them to lift herself high and come down fast on me, she buried me deep within in her sex. She kept rising and lowering, rising and lowering, the sound of our wet bodies striking each other filled the room, along with her grunts each time my cock hit her G-spot.

Her eyelids were heavy, jaw slack, as she used me to take herself higher…closer.

My hands wrapped around her waist to force the pace until she fell into the fierce thrusts of what we both needed. My fingernails trailing higher up her dress. I dragged the straps off her shoulders, allowing her breasts to bounce free. My lips found a nipple and sucked, moving from one to the other and feeling her sex tighten around me.

Rising and falling, rising and falling, Andrea becoming more frenzied, her moans drowned out by the sound of the water; our bodies squelching together.

Beneath those sprays we honored the Karma Sutra.

I fucked her from behind now, grabbing the bars above myself and using them for leverage to pummel her through her first orgasm. Next, with her spread-eagled on the bed and my face buried into her sex, I sucked the sweetness of her, tasting her sugary clit and feeling her arch her back beneath me.

We were two lovers possessed with each other, our bodies sliding and gliding effortlessly into every conceivable position, perfectly in-sync, her needing my affection to focus on her clit, to flick it just the way she liked, which was nice and slow - and then deliver a vigorous strumming to bring her closer still.

My balls ached for her touch.

Intuitively she reached for them and provided the massage they yearned for.

We were sex drunk.

Two lovers worshiping each other's bodies and exalting in *us*.

Slipping and sliding around that bed, being careful not to tumble off when our fucking became too vigorous. Our sixty-nine position enabled us to devour each other, both of us spacing out with pleasure as we delved into the sensual oral act, her sex soaking my face, the feel and taste of her sending me into rapture.

The bliss of limbs intermingled, our arousal at fever-pitch.

Above that melodic backdrop came our deep-throated groans. She slipped out of my grasp, moving on to raise her butt high.

Inside her, leaning over her, resting my head on her spine, never had such intimacy felt so sure, so real, so authentic.

I lay on my back again and brought her toward me, positioning her to lie along my front and face away from me, with my cock buried deep inside her, my hips a frantic piston beneath, ensuring the tip of my cock met her G-Spot with each strike. Strategically, I shifted us down slightly and eased her thighs open wider, supporting them in that position, holding them there so with that small adjustment of her pelvis, I ensured that one of those intense sprays of water was directed right onto her clit and stayed there.

"Yes," she stuttered breathlessly.

My thrusts continued slow and sure.

She became lax in my arms, overcome, tranced-out, my sweet sub needing to be taken higher.

And higher still...

My hand slapped across her mouth as she screamed her climax, her body shuddering, her thighs trembling, her head slack against my chest.

Her moans grew husky as she tilted her hips to take more of me.

Flooding her with warmth, we came together, both of us rocking perfectly and riding out these unraveling thrills, our orgasms owning us. We refused to come down, both of us held in a climatic suspension.

We settled like that for what felt like an eternity, with me firm inside her, that spray continuing to pound her sex and her moans proving she was savoring this endless pleasure.

As my erection swelled within her once more, I knew the startling truth.

We were perfect together.

The irony of an impossible conquest.

Reasoning with my belief that we wouldn't last had spurred me on to open myself up and let her in.

Only with an open heart could I have read hers and saved her.

I'd had nothing to lose.

Until now.

CHAPTER 19

HER LAUGHTER.

It was her laughter that made me smile and cracked through this hardened heart. And the way she grinned my way, that warmth reaching her eyes and lighting them up.

As we stepped out of the back of the town car, she looked so endearing in her disguise of short, white wig, those big sunglasses worn so elegantly, her jeans and T-shirt rounding out her casual camouflage.

Both of us were taking the biggest risk yet in order to slip into a restaurant together and get to the private table without her being recognized.

With my hands tucked inside my jeans, head down and baseball cap on, I feigned nonchalance as I followed the waitress to our table. It wasn't the autograph hunters we feared but those aggressive paparazzi, or a waitress with a tip for the press. We were risking a crowd of photographers gathered outside when we left but this need for normalcy felt worth it.

After our spectacular lovemaking back at The Lux Spa, we were both relaxed and tension free as we settled into our private corner in *Mr. Crabster's Crabby House.*

We shared a look of triumph.

Andrea slipped off her sunglasses and placed them to the side of the table. I removed my cap and sunglasses and placed them beside hers.

She looked over at the roll of paper towel on our table.

"Well, as you love messy adventures so much," I said.

She reached for a menu, her gaze reading the list of food and then rising to take in the crowd around her - diners wearing plastic bibs and eating crab legs with their fingers.

Her face scrunched in a smile. "You did not."

"Revenge for that experience known to the world as water torture. I'm sure some human rights lawyer is busy trying to put a stop to Lux's illegal shenanigans."

"You loved every second."

"The second half wasn't bad."

"Wasn't bad?"

I shrugged. "Okay, it was pretty spectacular."

She feigned fanning herself. "That was the hottest sex I've ever had." She slapped her hand over her mouth. "I didn't say that too loud, did I?"

"Sure did."

The tip of her shoe met my calf.

"Hey."

"I know you like it."

I frowned at her playfully.

"Anyway," she said, "Pendulum was just as amazing."

"You're amazing, Andrea."

She blushed as she reached out to the tub on our left and examined the fine tools within, one for cracking open crab shells and the other for scooping out the meat. Her stare met mine questioningly.

A pretty Asian waitress closed in on our table and if she recognized Andrea she didn't say. "Have you had a chance to check out the menu?"

"We've been chatting," I said.

"You choose, Richard," said Andrea. "You've got great taste."

Taking my time I decided on a few dishes off the menu and ordered two Miller Lites. We were given our plastic bibs and I leaned over the table to help Andrea with hers, which really was just another excuse to touch her.

Our waitress headed off to place our order.

"Can I ask you a personal question?" said Andrea.

"Sure."

"Do you prefer L.A. or New York?"

"You backed out of what you were going to ask."

"That obvious?"

"Yes."

She blushed and sat back, her fingers tracing the edge of the table. "Okay. Why are you into this kind of stuff?"

"You mean seafood?"

She gave a crooked smile.

"I realized pretty early on I was into kink. Luckily for me I met Cameron during my early days at Harvard. He was a few years older and his tastes were sophisticated. He made sure those drawn to our lifestyle were protected."

"How?"

"He owned and ran a private club back then too." I leaned on the table. "He gave me my first submissive."

"Gave you?"

"It's a club term. She was equally into the scene. So there were no surprises."

"Do you have sex with the clients?"

My frown deepened as I thought through my answer. "We utilize a therapeutic technique that leans toward it. It's complicated. Certain clients receive individualized therapy."

"Way to avoid the answer, Richard."

"It's rare."

"Did you help Ethan?"

"We also offer confidential services."

"He was different after his treatment with you and Dr. Cole."

"He told you that?"

"Not in so many words. Ethan was crushed after his wife died…when she was murdered." Her gaze rose to meet mine. "He came with me to Florida. Our aunt has a house in Key Largo. She invites us out every year. The kids, there's about ten of us. Brothers and sisters and cousins. We swim, and sunbathe, rest and escape. And eat too."

"Sounds fantastic."

"It is. You can come with me if you like."

My gaze shot to hers. "You're going out of town?"

"After this shoot."

"Not sure that would be a good idea."

"Silly idea." She shook her head. "Not sure why I came up with it."

"Thank you, though, for thinking of me."

"I always am…I mean, I'm grateful for everything." She blushed wildly and reached into her handbag to peek at her iPhone. "Just got texted my call time tomorrow."

"What time?"

"Seven." She arched a brow. "Would you like to visit me on set?"

"I'm afraid I have work tomorrow. I'm helping a friend out with his portfolio. It really does require my full attention."

125

"Of course. Oh, I forgot to thank you."

"What for?"

"The *Doctor Who* mug." She beamed. "I'm too scared to drink from it in case it breaks."

"I want you to enjoy it." I cringed. "Those fucking Daleks scare the hell out of me."

We laughed hysterically.

"I'm glad you love time-travel as much as me," I said with a wink.

"Some things are easy to fall for." Her gaze stayed on me.

Remaining nonchalant, or trying to, I broke her stare and saw our waitress heading our way.

She placed two large plastic bags between us, both of them holding crabs legs, unpeeled shrimp and cobs of sweet corn. Andrea's giggles rose once more and she slapped her hand over her mouth when she realized how loud she'd gotten.

The food was drenched in garlic butter and as I snapped open a crab's leg for Andrea, juice trickled over my hands. I handed her the small red hook and watched her elegantly scoop out the crab meat. She popped it into her mouth and her face lit up.

I set about peeling a shrimp for her.

She picked one out of the bag herself, peeled the shrimp and handed it to me. We ate like this, taking our time to snap a crab's leg or peel a shrimp, and hand it to each other, both of us not caring about the messiness - in between sipping lime beer and chatting away.

"I'm just a girl," she said.

I sat back ready to listen.

"You make me feel like me. Ordinary."

"You're extraordinary."

"What I mean is when I'm with you I feel so relaxed."

"That's good."

"I suppose you can't go through something like that and not change."

"You mean face off with Joy?"

"Yes."

"By pushing beyond fear we master it. What seems terrifying before seems manageable."

"I'll have to be careful what I tell you in future."

"You did ask for my help."

"That was not what I had in mind."

"Should've been more specific."

Another tap with her heel to my shin.

"Richard, I can't believe no one has snapped you up."

"Well, I'm not easy to live with."

"Neither am I."

"Yes, you are Andrea. You're easy to be around."

"Perhaps we can remain friends when this is over."

"I believe I've taught you everything you need to know about my world."

"Yes, I suppose."

"Maybe we'll see each other at another charity event?" I tried to sound polite.

Don't do it, don't end this. Not now, not ever.

"Is this like our celebration dinner?" she muttered.

"It is."

"I suppose what we did back at Lux Spa was the best break-up sex ever."

"Not really break-up sex as we're not technically dating." I gave a nod. "More of a celebration of us."

"It feels a little unreal."

"I want to thank you." I pressed my hand to my chest. "It's been cathartic for me, too."

"How?"

"I'd ended a relationship before we met and needed time to heal. Being with you, time spent with you—" I chewed my lower lip thoughtfully.

"I want to see you again, Richard."

The other me, the one who didn't know any better, reached out for her hand and squeezed it and told her I wanted that, too.

The reasonable me said, "Andrea, we both know my past and your future would clash."

"I don't care about what people say."

"It's my job to protect you." I lowered my gaze. "This is a normal reaction to the impending end of a master's training. It's expected."

Her gaze stayed on mine. "You're wrong. We're amazing together. You and I both know it. Our chemistry is incredible. You're the one who taught me to face my fears and go after what I want."

My head and heart were doing summersaults and threatening to crash into each other and render me speechless.

The greatest love would mean giving *her* up and *her* letting go. Doing what is right for her. I'd proven once before I was capable of doing that with Mia, and now she was in her lover's arms and happier than ever.

Happiness and I had never truly understood each other. A mish-mash of moments caught when sadness was looking the other way.

Rallying my strength, I reached out and took her hand in mine.

"At least think about it," she said.

"We'd always be hiding from the press. You'd have to keep me a secret. That's not the kind of life I want - for you or me. I'm sorry."

"You're wrong."

"Excuse me." Our pretty Asian waitress appeared in a flurry, her face flushed, wearing an awkward smile.

"Yes?" Andrea peered up at her.

"Could I get your autograph for the bartender?" she said sheepishly. "He's a huge fan of yours." She looked over at me.

I gave Andrea a sympathetic smile.

She reached for a napkin and dried juice off her hands. "Of course. What's his name?"

In a haze of realization I watched what our friendship had done to her.

What *I'd* done to her.

Andrea's hands were shaking.

CHAPTER 20

SCARLET DOUBLED OVER in hysterical laughter.

"What?" I said mischievously.

She flopped down into my leather armchair. No doubt with my office door open everyone would hear her.

"Your first sugar scrub?" she said.

"The whole thing starts off like a form of water torture and the next thing you know you're wishing it would never end."

I'd never reveal how the second half of "the sugar treatment" went, but Scarlet was a spa addict and knew exactly what I was talking about.

"My first time," she said, "I thought I was going to drown."

"Don't let me drown…"

Andrea's aura seeped into my psyche and my thoughts carried me back to her. I'd not spoken with her for two days and it felt like years.

This, this was torture of my own making. Doing what was right felt so wrong. I ran my fingers through my hair not wanting Scarlet to see me like this - completely spellbound, head spinning. I'd long ago mastered the expression that life was fine, the impossibility of love calling me only to laugh in my face.

That open book by Chaucer was on my desk. Reading it had brought comfort.

Scarlet peered down at the note card and the book with Andrea's signature. "What a wonderful gift. Andrea Buckingham's a keeper."

I lowered my gaze.

She rose out of the chair and came over, wrapping her arms around me in a hug. "You can still be friends."

I played with a pen on my desk.

"Have you fallen for her?"

My gaze met hers.

Ethan Neilson strolled on in, his face drawn, his glare on me.

"Ethan," said Scarlet, pulling away from me.

"Sorry," he said. "Did I interrupt?"

"No, of course not," she said.

He didn't look convinced.

Scarlett tapped my arm. "I have a sub in the dungeon being prepared. She's an applicant for our new secretary. Thought we'd hire a worldlier assistant this time." She winked at me and then leaned toward Ethan and kissed his cheek. "It's great seeing you."

He gave a thin smile as he watched her leave. "Close the door, please," he told her.

"Good to see you, Ethan," I said warily.

Scarlet shut the door behind her.

He came at me swinging a punch and I caught his fist and deflected it, shoving him down into an arm lock.

"What the fuck did you do to my cousin?" he snapped.

I yanked his arm back. "Can you be more specific?"

He froze. "Let go."

"If you promise not to attack me."

"Let me go."

"Promise."

"No matter how much I want to."

"You're a D.A." I freed him and stepped back. "Aren't you meant to have self-control?"

He sprung up, staggered to his feet and I braced for another attack.

"You could have killed her," he said.

"I would never let anything happen to her."

"You don't exactly have a good past record of taking care of your lovers."

I flinched. "That was cruel."

"I referred Andrea to you so you could discuss the BDSM lifestyle. Not so you could drown her."

"If you're referring to the trip on the boat, she enjoyed it."

"You're out of your fucking mind."

"She had a breakthrough, Ethan."

"No, you don't. You don't get to compare what Cameron does to what you did with Andrea."

"It worked."

"All you did was scare her."

"Did she say that?"

"Of course not. She's too classy to share her feelings, unlike you."

I moved closer to him. "I was in the room, Ethan, when you had your breakthrough. Don't forget that."

"And I'll always be grateful. That doesn't give you the right to hurt anyone I love."

"I would never—"

"There's no good in anything either of you do."

"Not true. You hadn't had an erection in five years, Ethan. I saw to it that dry spell ended."

"I'm not discussing this with you now." Pain flashed across his face, probably the memory of his wife being shot through the head at point blank range right in front of him.

The subsequent carnage of a legal case gone awry, the culprit set free to walk the streets, right up until Ethan had found him. Shay had made it go away. And a brilliant and well-respected D.A. had continued his life as though he'd not repaid his wife's murderer in kind.

No matter how much empathy I had for this man, I'd not let him off the hook that easily.

"As far as I recall," I said softly. "Your cock was in my hand when it got hard after years of impotence."

"And yet you say you're not gay?"

"Even when you came in my hand." I arched a brow. "So, technically, that would make you gay too."

His lips trembled. "Are you trying to undo all Cameron's hard work?"

"Hard being the operative word."

"Fuck you."

"*My* hard work, Ethan. I was in that room with you for a week, too. We ordered in pizza, for God sake. I stayed right beside you through the entire therapy. Remember that?"

He slumped in a chair and covered his face with his hands. "I should have had you both arrested."

"Love you too, Ethan."

"Why does it have to be this way? Why do we have to be pushed to the edge of madness to find our way back?"

"Because our pain refuses to budge. We have to outwit it. Outsmart it. Have the courage to face off with a greater fear."

What Cameron had accomplished with Ethan was a miracle. The man had been a mess when he'd come to us, underweight, unable to sleep for fear of that recurring dream finding him, and that haunting face of the man he'd murdered a frequent visitor in all its nightmarish gore. Cameron had healed Ethan's psyche and set him free.

And I'd been right there beside him to witness the miracle and aid in its revelation. A profound freeing of a soul and a renewing of a manhood.

That young ambitious man who'd presented as a D.A. in Cameron's office years ago, and threatened to shut down Chrysalis, had seen firsthand the benefit of the place. He not only dropped his investigation but ended up a member himself, allowing Cameron's genius to continue to save those around him. The House had overcome yet another threat. How frequently our enemies became our friends, those who spewed hate inevitably bowed at our feet and begged to be embraced by our elite foundation. Ethan had followed in the trail of other great men who'd doubted us.

Since then he'd been our greatest advocate - his quality of life improving and that fire that once burned within such a brilliant mind reignited, his passion refreshed.

"I was always scared of it," he whispered.

"Cameron knew," I said. "He knew your attitude toward sex was compromised."

"He made me see it's not dirty, or…"

"Remember what he told you, Ethan. Sex, as so perfectly explained in Abraham Maslow's hierarchy of needs, is normal, a beautiful thing. When we embrace our sexuality we push away our existential angst and truly shed our anxiety so we're free."

"Self-actualization."

"There's no shame in it."

He shook his head, obviously conflicted.

"Ethan, what we do here is miraculous work."

He sprang up. "How dare you try your dangerous technique on my cousin? You should have sought my permission first."

"I would never let anything happen to her. I care for her deeply."

"I blame myself."

"You know me better than this." I stepped forward and grabbed his arm. "I love and respect you, Ethan, and I know you feel the same way about me."

"This is messed up."

"Andrea means the world to me."

"Cameron goes out of town for five minutes and you wreak havoc."

"Andrea told me she felt the benefit of facing her fear," I whispered. "She needs to stand up to Mubarak."

"You should have turned her down when she asked for emersion."

"I've treated her well. Focused on pleasure, mostly."

Because of her aversion to pain.

"Mostly?" he muttered.

"I'll talk to her."

"No, I'll talk to her. Ask her forgiveness for ever mentioning your name."

"What has she told you?"

"She's back on set. Throwing herself into her work. Trying to salvage what's left of her self-respect."

"I didn't hurt her."

"You put her in the water with an eighteen-foot shark, Richard."

"I wanted to be the one to tell you."

"TMZ's running a feature on her new mysterious boyfriend. Shay will throw a fit."

I swallowed hard. "Did they say my name?"

He shrugged. "Look, I'm here to take you to over to Warner Brothers."

"Where Andrea's filming?"

"Her publicist wants to meet with you."

"Why?"

"She's working on a strategy to make this whole thing go away."

The ache in my chest worsened. "You mean me?"

CHAPTER 21

THE INTRODUCTIONS WERE brief.

Megan Banks met Ethan and I outside Andrea's luxury trailer, and we made the short journey up the steps and went inside.

Megan wore the fierce demeanor of an East Coast businesswoman, bleached blonde hair in a French plat, shiny purple silk shirt and a pencil skirt to her knees, tight and restrictive, like her expression.

Looking around I caught sight of how Andrea had made this little space welcoming. Cushions of every color on the couch, a small fridge and Perrier bottles lined up neatly along the small kitchenette, a vase full of lilies. Seeing them made me question who'd given them to her, and I felt an unfamiliar pang of jealousy. I mused that such an emotion was perfectly normal, we'd bonded after all, as lovers do, my imagination soothed me with the conclusion she'd bought them herself.

Near her bed sat that large blue *Doctor Who* Tardis Police Box mug.

She had a rose-patterned duvet she covered herself with when she took naps, no doubt her way of enduring the long production hours and her need to be fresh for each take. I'd made her believe I'd not cared for her profession but in reality I'd seen the truth behind the veil. The grueling hours, the constant hounding by fans or stalkers with cameras who called themselves journalists, and more impressive still was how far she pushed herself to be perfect for everyone around her.

Megan Banks' death glare stayed on me and I was grateful when it shifted to Ethan. Had this been any other day under different circumstances visiting Warner Brother's back lot might have been considered a fun day.

That East Coast accent came on strong, pure New York, pure Megan Banks fueled on caffeine and ambition. She told me she'd been Andrea's publicist from the start of her career, she also shared that their business relationship had turned into a deep friendship. Megan and Andrea were best friends and Megan would do anything for her.

Megan shot me a knowing look.

"Andrea's smitten with you," she admitted.

"I'm very fond of her," I said. "She's very special."

"Are you in love with her?" she asked.

I looked to Ethan for support.

His expression hadn't changed from when we were back at Enthrall. That look of defeat filled with empathy and that arched brow to warn me the strike was coming.

As though on cue, Megan went for my jugular. "I'm afraid your current profession isn't going to fly, Mr. Booth."

"Excuse me?"

"I work tirelessly to keep negative press away from Andrea. It's not difficult, not really, not if she continues to surround herself with people with integrity. There's an art to ensuring her name remains untainted."

I stood tall, quietly warning myself not to be drawn into her drama. "What are you trying to say?"

"Should it become known that Andrea is fraternizing with a man of your profession—"

"You mean stockbroker?"

"We both know you're not a stockbroker, Mr. Sheppard."

She'd used my real name like a bad move on a chess board.

I folded my arms across my chest. "Actually, I handle several clients' portfolios—"

"Megan," said Ethan, "Richard understands the delicate nature of Andrea's reputation. He's agreed to extricate himself…"

And so it went on.

Andrea and Ethan talking over me, the discussion morphing into accusations of how I'd taken advantage of Andrea's delicate psyche and the conversation circled the drain fast as they delved deeper into my family history. Megan's emphasis on how such a connection with me would ruin an actress of her caliber.

"It's better if you let me talk," snapped Ethan.

Trying to defend myself had riled up Megan's ugliest side, apparently.

She'd screamed at me to. "Shut the fuck up."

Taking a moment to recover from her outburst and drawing on my Zen, I kept my voice calm. "I'd never to anything to hurt her." I glanced over to the door to the outside.

God, these trailers were small. Suffocating.

Megan calmed a little. "Ethan has assured me you are essentially a good man, Mr. Sheppard."

"Please, call me Richard."

"I'd like to believe you are, a good man that is, unlike your father." She might as well have stuck one of her over-manicured fingernails in my carotid.

It was never meant to last, I reasoned.

You were never meant to like her quite this much.

The signed agreement was fulfilled. The time limit reached. The submissive in question having benefited from the brief and yet startlingly profound experience.

"To be frank, Mr. Sheppard, it's over."

Trying to convince myself this was the truth and that I'd not developed feelings for this woman who seemed to belong more to others than herself, a lover who'd come into my life and swept me up into the storm of her existence, her love pure, her sweetness enduring, her affection healing.

All this time I'd arrogantly believed I was helping her.

"So we have an understanding?" said Megan, her voice coming from far off.

"Yes," I heard myself reply.

"Well, I'm glad you're reasonable at least."

I frowned at her. "At least?"

"Yes, most men would see her fame and money and not let go so easily."

"It was never about that," I said. *She came to me.*

Ethan rested his hand on my shoulder. "Let's go get a drink."

I gave a reluctant nod.

Perhaps this was how it was done? When Andrea was over a man she got Megan to do her dirty work. Perhaps I'd never know.

"Please explain this to Andrea for me," I said softly.

Megan gave a thin smile.

"Tell her…" I searched for the words, maintaining an air of nonchalance.

"I'll tell her to focus on her career, Mr. Sheppard, as I always do."

With Ethan close behind me, I made my way down the short steps of the trailer. I wanted off this lot.

Hell, I wanted off this planet.

"I'll handle the press," said Megan, hurrying behind us.

Probably more for Ethan's sake than mine.

"We appreciate that," he said.

My legs froze when I saw that beautiful face coming toward me, a well of panic rising in me that I'd have to endure another awkward exchange - this time with Andrea.

I braced for the impending coldness between us.

I'd have to explain why I was here. My jaw clenched and my chest constricted.

Andrea stopped suddenly when she saw me. Sienna was by her side. A few words were exchanged and Sienna scurried away, throwing me a passing nod as she went.

I went to apologize for being here.

Andrea ran toward me and leaped into my arms, wrapping her arms and legs around me, hugging me tight. "I'm so happy you're here."

CHAPTER 22

"WE'LL ONLY BE a moment," Andrea told Ethan and Megan, as she gripped my hand and pulled me up the trailer steps.

With no choice but to hurry behind her I threw Ethan a reassuring smile while trying to avoid the glaring daggers from Megan.

I shut the door to the world outside.

Her face was flawless, that stark makeup applied with perfection and extra heavy for the lights. That short peach-colored dress so feminine, her dark hair curling around her shoulders.

"You changed your mind?" she said.

"So unlike me." I forced a smile, my heart aching that I was about to deliver the deathblow.

"I can't stop thinking of you." She fell to her knees and went for my zipper.

"Wait."

She was fast, too fast, her hands bringing me out of my pants and massaging me, the tip of her tongue running along the head of my cock.

"We need to talk," I reasoned breathlessly, trying to fight this need to break away, trying to fight this need not to.

She slapped my hands away when I tried to stop her.

Thoughts swirled, my senses sparking—

Andrea was deep-throating me and my hardness grew in her mouth. She owned me, captured me completely and I became her willing prisoner. When her hands cupped my balls and squeezed, I flinched.

"We should talk."

"We are." Her mouth took me all the way in again, her hands now on my ass and drawing me into her with a fierce rhythm.

I wanted to tell her this was not the best idea, knowing that our judge and jury were waiting outside for us to exit in the next minute or so to prove this bad boy had done the right thing.

A shiver ran up my spine. My body rigid, my mind exploding with this swell of pleasure, finding my way back from this was impossible. The more I fought it the greater the anger raged for those who told me this was wrong when it felt so right - *she* felt so right - the more my cock hardened and ignored my silent plea.

My hands reached out on either side and gripped the walls, my knuckles white, my hips falling into the rhythm she commanded, the sounds of her wet mouth suckling, her soft moans of pleasure proving she needed this just as much as me.

"Andrea, stop, please, otherwise I'm going to come."

Her soft moan echoed; she hummed around me.

My head fell back and that vulnerable side I suppressed rose begging me for this, to let her be, let her have whatever she wanted. The rising bliss sending ripples of nirvana through me and making my muscles tight, my biceps flinch, my fingers tremble with tension.

This was freedom. This had been my way all along. In letting my guard down just long enough to train her, I had let this incredible woman in.

I was falling fast.

Freefalling.

I moaned her name.

My warmth spurted into her mouth and she swallowed me, her frenzied laps and kisses revealing her passion, her own need, her eyes peering up and meeting mine in that exquisite submissive way of hers.

She remained kneeling at my feet, head bowed, that bite to her lip proving she'd hoped she'd pleased me. "Thank you, Master. I needed that more than you know."

My jaw slackened in surprise.

And I was fucking unshockable.

I lifted her up and carried her over to that small couch, throwing cushions to the floor, and not caring where they fell. I slipped to my knees, hitched up her dress and buried my head between her thighs, pulling her panties out of the way and suckling her sex, knowing this was the last time I'd taste her and wanting her to know how much she meant to me.

She widened her thighs, her hands grabbing a fist full of hair and pulling me into her.

"I need this," she moaned, "Richard, please don't stop."

My tongue was fucking her now, my thumb on her clit, circling. She shivered against me, her groans rising and I slapped my hand over her mouth to quiet her scream when she came, my strumming taking her through another climax. Her back arched, her breath coming in heavy gasps of desire, her thighs trembling, that throaty moan as she came again.

She cupped her face with her hands.

"Come here," I whispered.

She sat up and wrapped her arms around me, her head resting on mine, her short gasps causing her body to tremble.

A knock at the door.

"We'll be right out," I said, and kissed Andrea's shoulder.

"Just need a few more minutes," she added.

I rose up on the couch beside her. "You look beautiful."

"I'm made up like a pancake."

"That's why you taste so good." I grinned.

"I missed you so much."

"It's good to see you."

"More than you'll ever know."

I took her hands in mine. "We've always been honest with each other."

"Yes, I love that about us."

I lowered my head trying to find the right words.

"What's wrong?"

"At the beginning of our agreement we agreed to a time limit."

"I've been thinking of that, too."

"Oh, okay. Good."

"Let's forget that silly contract."

"That's not necessarily a good idea."

She looked away.

"This is not what you think it is," I said.

"Then what is it?"

"Please, hear me out."

She gave a wary nod.

"This is why you have someone like Megan in your life, to protect you from scandal. What would people say if they knew you were with the son of the man who brought New York to its knees?"

"Are you here to end us?"

I squeezed her hands. "You've worked so hard to be seen as America's sweetheart."

Another knock.

"Please," I snapped.

Andrea grabbed my hands. "We'll find a way. I know we will."

"I'm not sure—"

The door opened and Sienna stepped in with a flushed face and a nervous fluster. I assumed they'd sent her in.

She waved the script she was holding. "Sorry to interrupt."

I clenched my jaw in frustration. "Tell Megan we'll be right out."

Sienna looked at Andrea nervously. "Mr. Mubarak's ready for you."

Andrea leaped to her feet. "Were they calling for me?"

"Yes," said Sienna.

Andrea fell against my chest. "Come with me."

"On set?"

She looked up at me knowingly. "We need to clarify a few things first."

Self-conscious of Sienna, my words slipped away and I gave a reluctant nod.

I'd escaped the impending fallout inside the trailer only to be greeted with Megan and Ethan's false smiles.

"Richard's going to watch me film," said Andrea, pulling me behind her.

My mouth opened but no words came out.

Despite the annoyance of being hounded away, I knew they were right. My personal life was all over the map and ill-suited for someone hoping to keep the public's affection. This baggage I'd never be able to shed would always haunt me like a recurring nightmare.

This was where true love was tested. Not on the whitewashed sands of walking lovers but in the trenches of life where one chooses to do the right thing.

I gave Andrea's hand a tug. "I'm afraid I can't stay, Andrea. I have to get back to work."

She turned and smirked up at me. "We'll chat between takes. I'm filming an emotional scene. It will help me to have you here."

"I really must go."

"Don't rattle my process." She winked.

She bounded along in that playful feminine way of hers, dark locks flowing, and all those fun times we'd spent together came flooding back, our memories few but each and every one cherished. She'd lifted me out of a slump and I owed her this at least.

Megan and Ethan stalked close on our heels and we entered the stage and went on through yet another heavy door.

Andrea pointed upward to the red light in an oval box. "When that's lit up and spinning you have to be quiet. Put your phone on silent."

Trailing behind her I worked on my phone, my fingers sliding across the screen to shut it off. Andrea walked confidently ahead of me. She received a wave here and there from the crew and she waved back. She seemed to know everyone's name and their faces lit up as she greeted them.

Behind the veil of filmmaking all glamour slipped away as the truth was soon discovered in all its dusty backstage reality. During the grueling long days their technical brilliance became more of an endurance test as the impressive stamina of the crew played out. You could see it on their faces.

We walked through the vast, dark stage, cold from hours of air conditioning and stepped over wires and cables and props strewn on the floor, posing as hazards. Tall wooden stands that when rounded proved they were hiding realistic window frames, walls and doors that appeared so real, and just beyond us sat the main set in the center.

A city apartment with all the touches of luxury, like that elegant artwork hung on the walls, the sleek lines of modern furniture from talented decorator's, the vast, long glass window overlooking the dramatic skyline of Manhattan.

Staring in awe I shook my head at the spectacular view. The same one I'd enjoyed all those years when I'd had a penthouse in the Upper East Side.

Andrea introduced me to the set designer, Brandon Zenon, and told me they'd worked together on another film, back when they were both starting out. They both shared Florida roots, she went on to say.

"We project the real background via laser," he explained. "It gives the vista an authentic perspective."

"Impressive." I watched him navigate the software on a laptop.

The way he centered the fifty foot image on the back screen, the profoundness of detail in that digital projection that made up the view.

"It really does appear real." I admired the panoramic landscape.

"We have a generous budget," he said, and turned back to chat with one of the cameramen who was strapping a Glidecam Smooth Shooter to himself for a stabilized shot.

Andrea guided me over to a dark corner where a line of TV screens rested before five chairs, and she told me this was called the video village. Andrea's name was on the back of one of the chairs - as were several of the other cast members. Mubarak's empty chair sat on the end.

Andrea squeezed my arm. "You can watch from here."

I gave a nod and turned to see Ethan and Megan standing a few feet behind us.

Andrea lowered her voice to a whisper. "Pivotal scene, my character Rose tells Jax she's ready to become his submissive."

My face flushed as my imagination placed me firmly in Jax's shoes and then a rush of happiness flooded my veins as I thought of Andrea.

What the fuck was that?

It didn't exactly help that she'd had my cock in her gorgeous mouth just ten minutes ago.

Andrea knocked my arm. "Look, Jax even looks like you."

Blaze Fumero strolled on in with the confidence of a leading man, the actor was evidently taking a break from his Emmy winning TV show to star alongside Andrea on this feature. He took center stage on the set and sat on the couch. He was swarmed by makeup artists and other members of the crew who tended to him.

Self-consciously, I patted my hair down though it was Blaze's hair that was sticking up. He did kind of look like me in a scruffy East Coast way. I liked to think of myself as a little better put together, then reminded myself he was in costume and those ripped jeans and worn T-shirt were probably not a true representation of the heartthrob who had everyone flustered.

"They probably think you're his stunt double," said Ethan, his kindness returning.

Megan's protective stance hadn't changed and she looked like she was wound too tight, and needed to take herself a lot less seriously.

One night with one of my Doms and that bee-sucking expression would be wiped from her highly strung mouth.

"Wait here, okay?" said Andrea.

She left my side and headed toward the set. A few members of the crew swarmed her now. She greeted them with a professional air, a smile here, a nod there, her expression pure focus.

The crew scattered.

I looked around to see what had rattled them.

He strolled into focus. A large framed man, his expression sour, his small round glasses sinister, beige combat pants and jacket, his movement slow and deliberate. Jack Mubarak was even more intimidating in real life, his scowl revealing the kind of physical pain he wanted no one to know about and from his guarded walk I assumed it was his lower back.

He glowered at Andrea. "Nice of you to join us, Ms. Buckingham."

She shrank, her calm demeanor dissipating and though she hid it well to the others I'd gotten to know that flush on her neck, that uneasy way she lowered her gaze to peek beneath long dark lashes, the way she shifted her footing.

Our eyes caught and I gave her a comforting smile.

"Pictures up," someone shouted from our left.

The set went quiet.

"Camera's rolling," came the call.

A loud buzz echoed in warning.

The scene unfolded dramatically with Blaze and Andrea going at it in a full on argument, and me reminding myself they were acting. Several takes later and the grueling pace of maintaining tension seemed to wear on them both. I admired their focus.

Blaze forgot his lines again.

And again.

Collectively we all cringed on his behalf as Mubarak stormed toward him and went on a tirade. All those rumors of the kind of bad ass this director was seemed to be true, judging by the stark evidence before us. His vitriolic attack on Blaze was so severe a few of the crew walked off.

Andrea approached them to defend Blaze.

Mubarak turned on her.

It was ugly, a dark monologue on how the budget prevented him hiring real talent and their inability to fully invest themselves. From what little acting I'd seen, none of it rang true.

I stepped forward ready to defend her and was gently restrained by Megan.

Ethan grabbed my other arm. "You'll make it worse."

"You're going to just stand by and let him talk to her like this?" I said.

"He talks to everyone like this," explained Megan.

"I'm not just going to stand here—"

"Do you really want to fuck everything up for her?" she snapped.

I glanced around at the staff and they broke my gaze, possibly worn down from days of enduring Mubarak's tantrums, or just trying to get through this without getting fired.

"I need some air." I walked away and headed into a dark corner, glancing back to make sure Megan hadn't followed.

I turned my phone back on and speed-dialed Isaac Loftin.

His gruff voice answered. "Yes?"

"It's Richard," I said softly. "Did I wake you?"

"It's fine," he replied sleepily.

"Are you on the boat?"

"No, UCLA."

"Taking a nap in your office?"

"Was trying too. I'm lecturing in ten minutes to a bunch of undergrads who habitually text during my lectures. Trying to shed my grumpiness before I tackle the bastards. What's up?"

"You were going to email me the footage?"

"Could have sworn I did." I heard the sound of his laptop firing up. "I've labeled it top secret Booth project."

"I appreciate that."

"You might not want Andrea to see it. It's pretty shocking."

"In what way?"

He chuckled. "You kids were out of control."

"Chance of a lifetime."

"Maybe I'll show it to my students."

"Sure, whatever you want."

"Boy, do you have stamina."

"I like to think so."

"Just so you know we didn't leak the news you were both aboard the *Score Settled*. Maybe someone saw you together at the harbor? Still, Entertainment Tonight doesn't seem to know who her mystery guy is yet."

"Yet."

"Okay, well the file should reach you soon."

"Stay safe."

"Always, come visit us again soon. Don't leave it so long this time."

"I promise. Let me know if you need anything."

"Will do, Richard."

He hung up.

The file began its download.

CHAPTER 23

"GET THE FUCK off my set," snapped Mubarak.

Blaze stared him down.

The escalation of tension had reached new heights. Ethan was pacing and Megan was snapping at him.

"Where did you go?" Megan glared my way.

Ethan gave me a wary glance and he looked so conflicted, probably considering saying something, but, like everyone else, he feared making things worse.

"Maybe this is Mubarak's method?" I gave a casual shrug. "You know, his way to get the actors to dig deep."

"Shut the fuck up," hissed Megan.

From what I could tell Andrea was holding her own.

"I don't even know why you're here," seethed Megan.

I gave a polite smile, using this opportunity to prove she had no power over me. My focus returned to Andrea.

She stood before Mubarak, her arms folded across her chest, her stance confident.

"Please don't speak to me like this," she told him.

"It's my set, Ms. Buckingham," he replied sternly.

She gestured to the crew. "Our set too, sir. We're just as passionate at turning out a fine film."

"And yet your co-star can't remember his lines?"

"Well, if you didn't sit there in your director's chair sending daggers our way," she said, "it would be easier to focus."

"How dare you?"

"I'm merely explaining—"

"Do you like being on this film?"

"Of course. I've dedicated my life to living and breathing this part. I've immersed myself in this role."

"You're going to have to do better than that, Ms. Buckingham."

She pressed her hand to her chest. "I am Rose."

"Rose is brave, she's an inspiration—"

"I'm brave."

"This town is full of actresses ready for an opportunity like this."

"You can't fire me. We've started filming."

"I sent you away to find that fierceness, that life force. I needed you to prove you're capable of risking everything."

"I faced off with an eighteen foot shark for this!"

"Knowing you, Ms. Buckingham, it was probably a dolphin."

Silence.

The entire crew's attention focused on the enormous back screen digital projection. The New York vista had been replaced by the vastness of an underwater seascape.

Rippling reflected shards of light flooded the stage, that laser image now a murky blueness; an endless ocean - the muffled sound of bubbles and swirling sea water.

The stunning visual of two divers floating in a glass cage.

Hushed whispers from the startled crew, murmurs of confusion.

The shark's vastness rising from the deep and tracing through the water as the enormous fish approached the glass cage, her tale fast propelling all eighteen feet of her. A flick of her tale, that movement decisive, her gaping jaw wide, those serrated teeth exploring the glass.

Floating in the hazy space was Andrea, seemingly calm from the camera's vantage point, her arms wrapped around me in a hug and then breaking away in a moment of bravery, turning to watch Joy swim by again.

To some, we were brilliant explorers of the deep. To others, we were clearly out of our fucking minds.

"What is that?" whispered Megan.

"A Sunday afternoon," I murmured.

I strolled across the stage toward Jack Mubarak.

Shoulder to shoulder with him, I looked up at the screen. "It was damn cold at that depth. Joy Feast made you forget about that."

"Joy Feast?" said Andrea. "You told me her name was Joy?"

I grinned mischievously.

Mubarak stared up at the scene. "Andrea?" His intense hazel gaze locked on that impressive shark.

The visual detailed effect was so stunning this entire vast stage could have been underwater.

"Isn't she beautiful?" I smiled at Andrea. "Joy's thirty years old."

"The Ordovician period," muttered Mubarak.

I gave a nod. "Sharks have ruled the ocean for over 450 million years. You can see why."

"When?" he whispered.

"A week ago." I tucked my hands into my pockets. "Joy's jaw could have crushed that cage if she'd wanted too."

Andrea shot me a look and I shrugged.

"Andrea is your Rose, Mr. Mubarak." I pointed up. "She's brave. Daring. Honorable."

He stepped toward Andrea and cupped her face with his hands, staring right into her eyes. "Bring me that woman. Up there. Show me her."

Andrea's eyes watered and she gave a nod.

Mubarak stepped back and turned to the crew. "Can we get New York back up please?"

"Lights up," a crew member called out.

"Rolling," shouted another.

Andrea threw a smile my way.

I stepped back into the shadows.

"Andrea," said Mubarak, lowering his eyes at her. "Give me shark girl."

She gave a confident salute.

The filming resumed, the scene playing out again.

Stillness descended and the tension was no longer on what had unfolded but the seconds and minutes that followed, the heartfelt monologue that Blaze brought to the scene, the way his lips trembled in reaction to Andrea's outburst, the profoundness of love, and how one decision could bring a relationship to its knees.

Filming cycled through re-setting, makeup re-touches, and the playful banter between Andrea and Mubarak.

Andrea's giggled when her co-star shared a joke.

"This is where I leave," said Ethan, flashing a knowing glance my way. "It's the collaring scene."

My focus snapped back to the set. Andrea was leaning over Blaze's knee as they rehearsed what looked like a spanking. The young actor slid Andrea's hem up, hitching it above her thighs and his hand came down hard on her butt. Blaze looked over at the director's chair for Mubarak's approval.

A nod gave it and Blaze delivered several hard spanks; Andrea's moans echoed.

My feet were riveted to the ground as jealousy surged through me. *My* submissive was being touched by another man and his technique was not nearly as refined. Yet I'd allowed Cameron to train Mia.

She'd needed saving, needed gentle handling.

It was the uniqueness of a master and submissive relationship; I knew her body, predicted her needs, anticipated her desires. It was an intimacy unlike any other.

"Again please," Mubarak called over. "Let's film this one."

Megan nudged up against me. "Now would be a good time to leave, Mr. Sheppard."

"I go by Booth now."

"I don't really care what you call yourself. It's time to leave."

"I'd like to let Andrea know—"

"No, no, that won't be necessary."

I gazed at the TV monitor before us with Andrea's smiling face looking into the frame, a flash of happiness, her confidence shining.

Mission accomplished, I mused darkly.

"We'll release a statement," Megan whispered. "A spin on how Andrea's number one stalker had to be removed by security."

Bitch rested on my tongue but I resisted letting the word loose.

I chose my footing carefully, avoiding tripping on a wire or cable and further humiliating myself.

With a shove the heavy door gave way and I stepped through the outer door in a daze and burst into sunlight, shielding my eyes from the glare until I could get my sunglasses back on.

Emma threw me a wave.

Within minutes I was sitting in the back of the town car, gulping Perrier water and trying to forget the grungy way Megan made me feel. "Santa Monica airport, please, Emma."

She glanced in the rearview. "Are you going out of town, sir?"

"No, it's the pick-up for a skydive."

She held my stare. "Can I get you anything?"

"A way to change history," I muttered, and pulled out my phone, replaying that underwater footage and smiling at the madness of it.

Had the crew seen the shark attack the buoys, which happened minutes later, they'd have questioned my sanity.

That glass cage was a metaphor for my life.

The only way to free myself from those hounds of hell wanting their money back from my family was to give it to them. All I needed to do was reach inside my bank account and transfer the money back to them.

All fifty million.

I was destined to hide for the rest of my life.

Emma navigated us off the lot and we passed a crowd on the left, some of them holding up banners with Andrea's face on it and all of them seemingly hoping to catch a glimpse of their favorite star.

I'd been a class-A idiot to think there'd be any likelihood of us extending our friendship beyond what had been initially agreed upon. I was no different than all those fans on the sidewalk.

Fucking embarrassing.

Even with her hinting this was something she wanted to explore, I could never risk that kind of exposure. My father's legacy was front and center.

My past a death sentence to happiness.

I'd wanted to storm across that set and rescue Andrea, carry her back to her trailer and save her from all that superficiality, those false friends that weren't going to be there if her career went south.

Her strength inspired me to find mine.

I let out a long sigh of gratitude that I'd had this brief time with her. I cherished the feelings it bought.

"Sir?" said Emma. "May I put him through?"

"I'm sorry, what?"

"The call, sir. It's Dr. Cole on the line."

"Sure." I lifted my phone to my ear. "Cameron? Are you there?"

The line was quiet and I cursed, thinking I'd missed him. "Cam?"

"Where are you?" he said.

"Driving. Needed to clear my head."

"Skydiving?"

"On my way to the pick-up now."

"Be careful."

"Always. You need to join me. Though it sounds like you've got your own adrenaline junkie moves going on."

"That trick you pulled on my shares."

"When I tripled them?"

"I need you to do it again."

Seriously, Cameron was starting to sound like me. The man was on tilt and taking risks.

He whispered, "Quadruple it."

Silence wedged between us and something told me he was second guessing himself. I gave him the time to think this through and change his mind. Return to the kind of rationality he knew so well.

"Cameron?" I could swear I could hear him thinking, those brilliant cogs turning.

"Richard," he said. "Do your thing."

I shifted in my seat. "Maybe you need a more experienced broker?"

"You're the best there is."

"I don't know, Cam."

"No regrets."

"Promise."

"Of course."

We drove by a homeless man there on the sidewalk and I wondered what kind of regrets he carried, what things in life he'd choose to do differently if given the chance.

Turn back time.

Get her back.

Start over.

"Richard, are you there?"

"As soon as I get home I'll get on it."

He didn't need to know I had a driver.

"Pull over and buy from your phone," he insisted.

"I'm not sure. I don't like the sound of this, Cole. You seem a little..."

"Make this happen."

"You're really putting this kind of pressure on me?"

"I'm carrying this, Richard."

"Don't blame me if this goes tits up."

"If you pull this off—"

"It's impossible. You do realize that?"

"What one man can do another can do."

I think I might have told him that once. Or did he tell me? "What do I get out of it?" I said with a smirk.

"Other than the generous commission?"

"Yeah?"

"Name it. Anything."

"For reals, player?"

"You have my word," he said brightly.

His faith in me and what I could pull off was always a boon to my rattled self-esteem.

"Mia," I said. "I want her back. If I pull this off, she's mine."

I waited for him to tell me where to go. A Cameron comeback to shut me down.

Silence served as his reply.

I gave a shrug. "There's this shiny new stock coming out of Silicon Valley. An Asian company called Destiny-Horizon. It's skyrocketing. Want me to go for it?" I grinned at my mischief. "So we have a deal, Cameron?"

Staring at my phone, I realized the call had dropped.

Or maybe he'd hung up.

I didn't want Mia back, not really. Her fragility, her sweetness, felt like holding fine glass in my hands. Shards that threatened to slice into me and leave me bleeding.

Andrea Buckingham, however, was like holding a wild cat in my arms, one that taming could never destroy. The kind of woman no man could break. No matter how hard he pushed her. Or fucked her, for that matter.

A submissive of the highest order.

The appeal of how my life could have gone. The tease of happiness.

This life-changing daydream had ended.

CHAPTER 24

I'D PULLED OFF the impossible.

Staring at Cameron's computer screen I scanned the numbers. His stock had reached a net worth of twelve billion.

At my hands no less.

I rose out of this trance and blinked to better take in the data.

I'd placed him squarely in the running to be able to purchase over 90% of Cole Tea shares.

But we'd have to act fast.

Those shares were chum in the water for greedy bastards on the prowl for flailing stock. If we bought them all now I'd make Cole the owner and CEO of the company.

I knew well enough not to assume this was the plan.

This change of fate would mean a drastic difference to Cameron's life, but the business he was trying so hard to save would finally have a chance. His family legacy was hanging in the balance.

I refreshed my screen.

I'd spent the day working on his finances, munching on cookies that Pilar brought in, though so focused I'd only been half aware she was in the room when she delivered them, my coffee mug always topped off and piping hot.

This coffee haze raced through my veins like wildfire.

I pushed myself back from the desk and let out a crazed laugh.

Winston was busy exploring Cameron's office and now and again he glanced up at me as though asking, "Where the hell am I?"

"Feel the same way, buddy," I said. "Cole's trying to save an empire and we're in the trenches with him doing our bit."

Cameron had been gone for well over a week and I couldn't remember the last time we'd spent such time apart.

I went back to check on the current state of Cole Tea and Tempest Coffee shares and winced. The numbers were bombing. His dad would be devastated.

I had to talk with Cameron.

Dialing his number again I yelled when it went to voicemail. I texted Mia with a warning they needed to call me right away.

I called Tempest Tower, asking to be put through to the main office, and was put on hold. The unending music proved this call wasn't going to happen - a seeming stranger speaking with the CEO without prior notice was against policy, no doubt.

I'd been so caught up with carrying out Cameron's orders I'd not thought to check on my own shares. My commission for dealing with Cameron's portfolio was generous. More than I'd ever made before and I'd handled some big accounts over the years.

The realization hit me—

I dropped the phone and flew out of Cameron's office, running down the hall at breakneck speed and almost knocking over Pilar. I caught her and swept her back up to her feet, cupping her face in my hands and planting a big kiss on her lips.

She squealed with delight, blushing wildly.

Her laughter trailed behind me.

I sprinted through the foyer and burst through the large oak doorway, taking two steps at a time until I reached the most private sanctuary of Chrysalis - the stables. Dominic's voice carried down the hallway.

A wayward pony trotted by and I sent him in to fetch Dominic. I was in no mood to lower my energy to suit the stables, a calm and nurturing environment.

I was on fire and couldn't stand still.

I paced, waiting, walking up and down the corridor outside.

Dominic was berating a pony. Though from the moans coming from the stables he was using pleasure to get through to the petulant brute.

I resisted storming in and shouting at the man who'd badmouthed Dominic right back, but from the sound of it, Dominic had it handled.

Within a few minutes I was walking beside him in the garden. We rounded the pool and headed off away from the house.

"May I suggest less caffeine?" He smirked.

"Just hear me out. I've had this wild idea and I need your help to set it up."

"I'm at your command," he said in that elegant yet annoyed way of his.

"What if I opened up a recovery fund? I've recently come into some money. A lot actually, and I want to put it all into an account and help the families who lost their money in my father's Ponzi scheme."

"You're out of your mind."

"Can I do it?"

"It's feasible."

"You have to help me, Dom."

"Where's the money coming from?"

"I have a very wealthy client—"

"You made commission?"

"Yes."

"This dabbling in the stock market paid off, I take it?"

"You could say that."

His smile thinned. "I imagine you'd still be on Wall Street if it wasn't for your father."

"I'm not sure. I love it here. I love my home, my life…" I waved that off. "Do you think it's something we can do?"

"A gesture like that is always looked on with gratitude. There'll be some legal fine- tuning. Remember though, no good deed goes unpunished, so there'll be fallout and press—"

"I can come out of hiding?"

"Yes, I suppose you could."

I threw my head back and stared up at the sky, my heart surging with the realization that freedom was a real possibility.

"I'll put a financial proposal together and we can talk through it," he said.

I leaped forward and hugged him.

He patted my back, "Okay, cowboy, let's get you some mineral water. Your blood is ninety percent caffeine."

"I'm going to be free!"

"I'm going to give you one of Pilar's cannabis cookies."

"Pilar cooks with pot?"

"That naughty sub Arianna got her into it. The kitchen's the most popular place after a session these days."

"Drugs are banned."

"Well, there you have it. Arianna knows we love Pilar and won't fire her."

"And Arianna is Shay's sub—"

"So she's not going anywhere."

"I'll talk with them both." I scratched my head. "Better still I'll have Cameron deal with it when he comes back."

Dominic arched a brow. "*If* he comes back."

CHAPTER 25

TRYING CAMERON'S NUMBER again I settled back down in his office swivel chair.

I typed in the code to access his account, refreshing the screen where I'd left it.

His shares had skyrocketed.

Grinning like an idiot, I screen-captured the numbers for prosperity.

I hit Cameron's number and his gruff voice answered.

"Cole?" I said. "'Bout time. Where are you?"

"Tempest Tower," he said weakly. "My dad's signing over the company."

"What? Why?" I jolted up. "Cameron, are you okay?"

"Are you enjoying this?"

"What the fuck?"

There it was. His brilliant deduction that I'd probably placed him firmly on the fast track to run Cole Tea, and he hated me for it.

I glared at the phone. *You asked me to triple your shares, buddy.*

"Is Mia there? Put her on."

"Is this about her?" His voice sounded strained.

I rolled my eyes at that. "I knew you'd never give her back."

"I can't breathe without her." He let out a long breath. "Did you do this on purpose?"

Cameron was being pissy, with a little weirdness thrown into the mix.

I'd only ever seen him like this once before and that was the night he'd called off his engagement with Zie. Cameron had been so full of guilt he'd not slept for a week. And he was crap without sleep.

Still, maybe it wasn't all bad news.

"I just hope you're willing to live with the consequences." I smiled at the impending news I was about to deliver.

His family empire was salvageable and pride seeped in that I'd played a part. "Don't blame me when your life is turned upside down."

The line went dead.

I figured I could have worded that better.

Calling back, Mia answered, "Hello? Richard?"

"Everything's fine, Mia. Put Cameron back on."

Her muffled voice came through as she spoke to Cameron. "Richard, please tell Cameron to get some sleep. He's exhausted. He only listens to you."

"Richard?" came Cameron's gruff tone.

"When was the last time you got any sleep?" I asked firmly.

"It was never about the money," he said firmly. "It was about a greater purpose. And if this is your way of getting me to realize how much I love Mia, well bravo, Richard Booth Sheppard. She's worth more to me than anyone will ever know. I never meant to hurt you. I've told you that a thousand times. I've begged for your forgiveness. Know this - I will not give her up. Ever."

I opened my mouth wide in a silent scream, then shook my head and said calmly. "Yeah, I could hear it in your voice when I asked for her back."

Asshole.

"Cameron," I said. "Check your shares."

"I did."

His panic suddenly made sense. "You think we went with Destiny-Horizon?" I rolled my eyes. "God, I know you so well. Those looked like crap in the end. We went with Phoenix-Rise. You did give me free rein after all. They just went public—"

"You didn't lose my money?"

"Well, that explains your pissy mood."

"Richard?"

"I just made a shitload of commission thanks to you. We went through Charlie's. Thought it best to buy under your charity name and that way no one would become suspicious that Cameron Cole...are you still there?"

"We're still here," said Mia.

"Cam," I said. "I quadrupled it."

Mia squealed and it made me smile.

"I'm assuming you want me to buy every Cole Tea and Tempest Coffee share I can get my hands on and add it to your portfolio?"

Mia piped up, "Cameron says 'yes please.'"

I tapped the keyboard and officially purchased the shares I'd readied to buy.

I knew the kind of pressure Cameron was under and he'd never been drawn to business, not really, although I suspected he'd thrive in this world and we both knew what a double-edged sword this was for him. There was the chance he'd have to leave his beloved psychiatric practice behind and take up his rightful place at his brother's side and run Cole Tea.

There was no other way.

I finished with a click of the mouse. "Booyah, fuckers!"

Winston barked.

"Quiet, I'm trying to concentrate here. That's the only good thing about a rumor of a hostile takeover. People dump their shares."

"What does that mean?" asked Mia.

It was done.

"Boom bitches!" I leaned back.

"Speak to me," said Cameron.

"You just became the proud owner of Cole Tea. Well, ninety percent anyway. Not bad for a day's work."

"Richard, you're a genius," shouted Mia.

"Well, we know that." I grinned, reaching down to pat Winston.

"I have to get back to the tower," said Cameron.

The line went quiet.

Winston stared up at me and I scratched his head.

"Richard?" said a breathless Cameron.

"Still here."

"Richard! Thank you."

"What are you waiting for?" I said. "Go."

The line went dead and my best friend went chasing after his future with the usual passion and brilliance he gave to everything.

God, I loved that man.

His life would never be the same. Neither would Cole Tea, and the thought of what he could bring to his father's company made me swell with pride. They had no idea what they had coming to them. The company was about to be taken to the next level.

I felt a sense of retribution for all the damage my father had done.

Pushing away from the desk, I headed off to the kitchen.

Though tempted to celebrate with one of Pilar's "special" cookies, I meant to have a little chat with her in the near future. She'd no doubt been manipulated by Arianna.

Dominic's words haunted my thoughts - that Chrysalis wouldn't be the same without Cameron. Was I ready to run this place with the same ironclad fist that he had protected this sanctuary of eccentric souls with?

Yes, yes I was.

I was also free to love who I wanted.

My feet stuck to the marble floor as that thought raced through my brain.

I fled through the front door of Chrysalis, startling the valet by grabbing my car keys off him and sprinting to fetch my Jeep myself.

I leaped inside the Wrangler and sped away.

The journey to Doheny Drive was a blur, all I could think of was how I'd tell Andrea that I'd found a way for us to be together, a solution that would bring me out of hiding and make it easier for the public to accept me as her lover.

She'd be dating a stockbroker, after all, and Cameron had led the way of smoke and mirrors, proving he could have this life and still protect his family name.

The words I'd say to Andrea rose from my heart.

I'd thank her for freeing me, for being the one to save me. I'd finally be able to tell her what she meant to me. There were no more reasons to stay apart or deny that we even knew each other.

I punched the dial on the dashboard and Pearl Jam blared through my speakers.

The promise of happiness loomed larger than it ever had. All this angst, all this suffering fell away like the promise of spring.

I turned the music up.

Within the hour I was driving up Doheny, the twisting street toward her home.

Uneasiness settled in my gut.

Thirty or so paparazzi were gathered outside the front of her house. More photogs than I'd ever seen. I parked a little way up the road so they couldn't catch the number on my license plate, and parked.

I strolled back down the hill with my sunglasses on and baseball cap pulled low.

Standing beside one of the photogs as though I was one of them, I brought out my iPhone and texted.

"Hey, Andrea, are you home?"

"What's going on?" I asked the photographer beside me.

"Buckingham just disappeared inside," said the stout, grisly looking cameraman.

My gaze shot to the window. "She's home?"

He nudged his glasses up his nose. "We followed the lovers back from Tandem's Lounge."

A chill ran up my spine.

"They've been keeping it on the down-low," he added. "We knew something was up. She was in and out of restaurants with him, wearing that wig of hers. They were caught holding hands today coming out of Boho Bakery. You know, the Grove?"

"What? When?" My voice sounded strained.

"This afternoon."

"With who?" My stomach ached and my mouth felt dry.

"Blaze Fumero?"

"Her co-star?"

He peered up at me. "You don't read your own tabloid then?"

"How do you mean?"

"Blaze and Andrea have been a thing since they began shooting. The chemistry's off the charts." He lifted his camera to show me and I stared down at the time-stamped photo from thirty minutes ago. A snapshot of Andrea heading into the house with Blaze, his arm wrapped around her. The second shot had his hand on her ass.

"I just made fifty thousand after I got an exclusive with them coming out of a club."

"Where?"

"Sunset. Last night. They couldn't keep their hands off each other."

I wanted to punch him.

"What site do you work for?" he asked.

"Forgot my camera." I feigned I was going back for it and headed back up the street.

I struggled with my keys, trying to get them into the ignition, dizziness causing nausea to well in my gut.

Sadness stuck in my throat and I coughed to relieve it.

Andrea was an actress and there lay the rub, she'd master-classed her way into my life and I'd fallen for it.

Fallen for her.

Yet again I'd aced being wrong.

I was a goddamned expert at it.

CHAPTER 26

THE DECADANCE OF a party at Chrysalis - nothing came close.

Despite all this luxury, this brilliant revelry, I still missed Andrea. These three days without her felt like years.

It was time to put this soiree behind me and move on. Not that I had any choice. What I'd not accounted for was the slew of TV networks running the story of her romance with Hollywood heart-throb Blaze Fumero.

A constant reminder of what I'd lost.

Of what I'd never really had.

We'd healed each other in our own way. Touched each other's lives and changed them irrevocably. Andrea had proven to herself she was capable of facing off with anyone and that she had moved past her fear. And I felt ready to love again.

Maybe even take on a new submissive.

It would take time to select the right one. What would follow would be the appropriate interviewing and assessing of which woman would most benefit from my skills and which sub would serve my needs best - a symbiotic relationship of Yin and Yang.

I yearned for the one.

I was ready.

My chest tightened at the knowledge that it would never be Andrea. I missed her warmth, her ridiculous giggling, her button nose and those cute freckles. I'd raced through these weeks with my usual brand of wildness. Regret seeped in that I'd not savored her more. The thought of her lying in Blaze's arms made me cringe.

I shoved the pain away.

My thoughts came back to the present.

Life had almost returned to normal. I was surrounded by good people. My people. And my best buddy was back.

Cameron and I sat at the top of the stairs. We were both dressed in our tuxedos, our gazes taking in the view of the foyer filled with partygoers.

New guests trickled in the front door taking in the scene, dominants guiding their subs on fine chains, some forced to crawl beside their masters as they peeked up from behind masks proving their thrill. A few ponies had been gifted with release from the stables this evening and I caught sight of Jason Harris trotting through the crowd with that sweet sub Trixie perched on his back and secure on that fixed leather saddle, her expression blissful, cheeks flushed, her sex no doubt receiving a good pummeling as she rode him.

The sight of their happiness made all this more than worth it.

Dominic peered up from the shadows giving me a knowing look. It appeared that Trixie's master was out of town again, and the agreement for her to play with Dominic's permission had been granted.

Dominic's gaze slid over to Cameron and his expression flooded with grief. He was losing his director and the man who'd saved his life back during those years of depression, when he hid his predilections and denied his homosexuality. Cameron had guided him into the light.

And that was why our symbol was a chandelier.

The light streaming off those hundreds of crystals stood as a beacon to the lost and an uplifting comfort to the found, a manmade crafted sculpture of glass reflecting the profoundness of human sexuality. Our lifestyle sophisticated, hedonistic, and always welcoming.

I gave Dominic a comforting smile and he gave a nod of appreciation.

"La Traviata" by Giuseppe Verdi flooded in from the great hall, the music a backdrop for Arianna being showcased during a session in front of an audience. Shay was taking his sub through her paces, this, their reunion after his time spent in New York with Cameron.

Just ten minutes ago before meeting Cameron here on the stairs, I'd made sure the scene in the great hall was perfectly set. Arianna had been strung up naked in the center, her hands bound above her head and that table pulled close and covered with the toys and accoutrements of pleasure and pain that Shay was probably using on her now.

I'd left them to it and had come to meet with Cameron.

To the left of the stairs, a young couple who'd just arrived was so caught up with the decadent scene they'd just stepped into that they'd delved right into fucking against the wall. And, as expected, they'd drawn an audience. I recognized them as first-timers and my nod to

Dominic signaled they were permitted to continue; they were, after all, entertaining our guests.

Cameron's mood was one of resignation.

We'd shared so much good and bad over our lives, most of which we'd endured together.

And together we'd created this place from the ground up.

His leaving was something none of us could have predicted. Scarlet, Lotte, and Penny were distraught. I'd comforted them the best way I could, kept them busy, given them tasks and right now Scarlet was distracted with Cameron's new sub, preparing Mia for their first voyeur session.

I patted Cameron's back to comfort him. "We've had some fun times, haven't we?"

"The best."

"I'm going to miss you, Cam."

"Come visit."

"You bet."

"You do realize what you pulled off for me, don't you?" he said.

"You keep reminding me."

"You saved us."

"Yeah, well you saved me. We'll be waiting for you."

It was my time to rule, to take over the position of director, which I'd always been destined for and Cameron had groomed me for. A rush of excitement flooded through me. The games I'd design. The punishments I'd deliver. The pleasures I'd bestow.

Adrenaline raced through my veins and arousal sparked my senses.

I swiveled to face Cameron. "You know what impressed me the most?"

"Go on."

"Even after you believed I'd purposely lost all your money you still didn't hate me. That was enlightening."

"Apparently lack of sleep doesn't look good on me."

I leaned on his arm. "Losing your friendship would crush me."

"Never going to happen."

"Dominic's not taking it well."

His gaze found him in the crowd. "Look after him."

"Of course."

He reached over and took my hand, peeling open my palm and placing a gold key there.

My time to reign.

I smiled at him. "Never thought the day would come."

He held my gaze and just as we always did our words were shared without speaking. He trusted in me to run this house as well as he had, to place my own touch on our precious sanctuary.

"The Harrington Suite was always destined to be for the three of us," I mused, more to myself than him.

"I know."

"You haven't been in there since you caught Zie…"

We both knew this was a profound day for him, a healing step.

"Actually, I gave Mia a peek during her first tour," he admitted.

"Interesting."

He gave a knowing look. "Mia wants this."

"It may well be her last chance. Next thing you'll be running for office."

"Hardly. My hands are going to be full."

The large cage rolled into view and I took in the beauty of Mia inside, naked and wrapped in fine chains, her mask hiding her face, but I knew those blue eyes, that small pale frame, her stark fragility proving she needed a master willing to analyze every action, guide her gently through each session and treat her with the kind of patience I never had.

I'd go for a well-trained submissive next time. One willing to perform in any way a director saw fit. As my mistress she'd need to set the precedent of how subs behaved.

My body warmed with the thought of the mystery woman, a physical validation as I scanned the foyer for prospects.

The memory of Andrea's face intruded on my thoughts.

A wistful musing as I recalled the first day we met, the way she bravely flung herself at my feet, her breaking into my home in search of resolution, and the way she'd stood up to Mubarak, proving she'd found it.

There was no room for sentimentality. Tonight I'd do my best to find a way to forget Andrea, let her go.

If I was going to be accepted as the new ultimate Alpha I would have to assert myself with the same authority Cameron always had. He'd taught me well and prepared me. I'd deliver the same fairness. Rule with an ironclad fist and with an open heart.

I flicked open my cufflink. "Shay's taking the night off."

"Yes."

"Will he be in there?" I asked. "Watching you?"

"No."

164

Relief swept over me.

"This session with her," he said cautiously. "Now that it's here…"

"The art of the performance. Proving just how sacred sex really is."

"I don't want you in there, Richard."

"I'm actually planning on a threesome."

He widened his eyes in surprise. "Shay and Arianna?"

"You're my inspiration."

"Let Shay win sometimes."

"I'll take it under consideration." I nodded toward the foyer. "Here's your girl."

He gave a pat to my shoulder and I beamed up at him.

"God, I'll miss you." Cameron made his way down the stairs.

I took in the scene of Chrysalis's foyer, looking so beautiful beneath the yellow dimmed light. Pride settled in my gut that I was inheriting the responsibility of this manor. I made a silent vow to make Cameron proud, to make everyone proud.

I descended the steps and made my way back to the great hall.

Crowds mingled here and there, talking, laughing, the occasional guest throwing a smile my way. I knew most of them. This would soon change. I'd come to know each and every member here and Cameron's files would become my own.

A wave of excitement that my time had come to reign.

Where Arianna had stood was now merely unclipped handcuffs hanging from the ceiling. A circle of blue irises were strewn at the base of where she'd been standing. They trailed toward the back of the hall, hundreds of fresh petals leading the way. Shay had scattered them for her in a romantic tease.

They stopped at the doorway leading to the dungeons.

I gave a smile at Shay's complexity, his ability to run a dynamic security business and keep us all safe. I admired his gentler side, the part of him that made him perfect for Arianna.

Through the door, I followed the trail downwards along the curve of the stairwell. The chill of the dungeons made my forearms prickle. I strolled down the hallway until I found the only dungeon with a door open.

I entered the small voyeur room and found Scarlet, Lotte, and Penny in there sipping champagne, seemingly about to enjoy a dungeon scene through the one-way glass.

As I stepped inside I saw Ethan, who was also dressed in a tuxedo, his mask tucked into his jacket pocket. He welcomed me in.

From here the view of the dungeon was muted. Its lighting so low it made it difficult to see beyond a few feet, but I picked up some faint movement in the corner, a couple talking.

Straining to see into the darkness, my eyes adjusted to the scene beyond the glass.

That was not Arianna. Even with her back to me I could see that.

The woman was tall and curvy, a brunette that looked nothing like Shay's inked-up sub. She looked like...

Cruel thoughts drenched my brain, the idea that it was *her.*

The scene was minutes from starting, a sub being readied for her master.

Shay was focused on securing her to the central, gold crystal chandelier, raising her wrists, bound in black leather cuffs. Those attached fine chains dangling and easy to break from.

"Where's Arianna?" I said.

"We have a new member," said Ethan, shrugging off my question. "Looks like she's almost ready."

My gaze snapped back to the glass.

He patted my back firmly.

I tried to shake off this yearning, not wanting to show just how hard I'd fallen. Just how hurt I'd be if I were mistaken.

"You have the key?" he asked.

I reached into my pocket and withdrew the one Cameron had just handed me, the symbol of my impending rule.

Or was it?

My gaze flew back to the room.

Ethan pointed to it. "The key for the new dungeon."

My frown deepened.

"The last contract Cameron signed as director is her member-ship," he said.

"Contract?"

"Your new submissive."

"You chose for me? Cameron chose her?"

Because she looks like *her?* I tried to comprehend their idiocy.

Ethan gave a shrug. "I'll see you later in the garden? We'll crack a bottle of Bolly. You'll make a fine director, Booth." He strolled out, securing his mask as he went, and then tucked his hands into his pockets.

It's not her, my heart warned, *it could never be her.*

Ethan didn't want me anywhere near her.

My heart raced, thoughts scattering.

Scarlet and Lotte threw me a big smile.

"Go claim her," Scarlet said.

Is it really her?

My stare moved over to Lotte.

"We all love you so much, Richard," she said. "You deserve her."

I sped out of there, bolting down the hallway and flying through the door into the dungeon.

Shay stepped back. "She's ready for you, sir."

God she was stunning.

Soft yellow light from above shimmered over her nakedness.

Dark curls tumbled over Andrea's bare shoulders, her tiny thong her only clothes, breasts pert, nipples erect, abdomen strewn with the same fine chain that had been used to secure her above to that delicate low-hung chandelier. Her arms taut above her, her chestnut gaze full of yearning and hope.

Time stood still and in a dreamy haze I approached her, only vaguely aware Shay had left.

"You have an uncanny way of breaking into places," I said.

"You have an uncanny way of seducing your subs."

"I thought Ethan didn't want us together?"

"He knows how I feel about you."

"Blaze?"

"What about him?"

"Your lover? The photos—"

"It's a ruse. He's gay and needs to look like he's not. Megan also believed it would pull the attention away from you should any rumors have leaked."

"You're not lovers?"

She laughed. "Your more his type, Richard."

"The press? All staged?"

"Yes. I can't think straight without you. I need you in my life."

"Shush." I touched her lips. "You didn't text me back?"

"Because I thought you didn't want me, not really. You left the set without saying goodbye. I thought I'd disappointed you."

"Never"

"You kept telling me we couldn't be together. I tried to believe it."

My fingers traced that curl of hair clinging to her neck and she rested her head into my palm.

"I had lunch with Scarlet," she said. "We talked. A lot. Mainly about you."

I gave a smile at how fiercely loyal my dominatrixes were…like sisters.

"I want this. I need to be yours." Andrea peered through the glass. "Scarlet told me you feel the same way?"

"Yes, of course."

She raised her chin proudly. "Ethan showed me your press release. The fund you set up?"

"My brothers are helping out. Cameron, too."

She sucked on her bottom lip. "We don't need to hide anymore."

"We'll have to keep your membership secret."

"You always do that so well here."

"You're in my new dungeon?"

"I am."

"Maybe we should test it out?"

Her mouth quirked. "What do you have in mind?"

I cupped her face with my hands and kissed her fiercely, my tongue forcing hers to submit. My body ached for her, even with her this close, and I wrapped my arms around her waist and buried my face in the crook of her neck, knowing the sacredness of this moment - of her.

"Do you accept me," she whispered, "as your submissive?"

"Yes, of course."

"Believe in us. That's all I'm asking."

I raised my head. "I thought I'd lost you."

"Never, we belong together. Don't fight it anymore."

"I'm never letting you go."

"My whole body's alight." She glanced up at the chain and the crystal chandelier. "This is where I belong."

I kissed her forehead. "How are you so damn strong?"

Her smile widened. "Because you taught me how to breathe underwater."

CHAPTER 27

One Month Later

A WARM OCEAN wave rolled over my feet; the gentle lapping sound soothing me.

This private, deserted beach had given me time to think clearly without the usual distractions - all of them of my own making. I'd been running to keep the pain at bay.

I realized that now.

I blinked against the rising sun.

Racing through my existence, I'd tried one way or another to push myself through life-threatening sports and yet here I was now, slowing down after all this time, standing still with my toes buried deep in golden sand and my trouser legs soaked; my mind quiet, peaceful.

Cameron had only been able to take me so far toward this peace. I'd had to walk the rest of the journey myself, and only when I was ready.

All that time invested in Cameron's business had turned my own life around. The commission from stocks had made me a small fortune. And I'd given it all away, invested in a trust fund for those New Yorkers who deserved it more than me.

I was still wealthy by anyone's standards, a millionaire with a growing portfolio that would always ensure I lived well. And my salary as director of Chrysalis was more than generous. I loved that grand manor and everyone who worked there, all of them accepting me with open arms as their new boss.

The news of Cameron and Mia's engagement had actually brought me comfort and knowing they were in the thick of planning a Cole wedding made me smile. My dearest friends had a bright future together. They deserved to be happy.

Those frequent calls from Cameron were reassuring, knowing he was thriving in New York. Mia had settled in, he told me, and Henry visited the office from time to time, but Cameron was firmly at the helm of Cole Tea. His father had retired knowing the family legacy was in good hands.

While I mulled over this revelation I sensed her.

Staring toward the blue ocean, I felt her arms wrap around my waist.

The wafting scent of water lilies enveloped me - Andrea's delicate perfume.

"I was wondering where you were." She hugged me tighter. "I woke up and hated not seeing you next to me. I had Winston help me find you."

I gave a fulfilled sigh.

My sweet mutt had no idea he was thousands of miles from home. He stood beside Andrea's feet, panting away, all sweetness and trust. He padded closer to sniff my foot.

"I'll feed him."

"Already fed." She laughed and handed me his tennis ball.

I took it and beamed a contented smile her way, throwing the ball high into the air. It landed in the water.

Winston dived in and swam after it.

With an arch of a brow I gave Andrea an amused look.

We stripped off our clothes and left them behind on the beach as we waded into the warm water, laughing as we went.

Skinny dipping, snuggling, riding the waves.

Making love beneath the water, arms wrapped around each other and keeping the rest of the world at bay.

Later, we returned to the house. This vast, ten-bedroom Mediterranean home belonged to her aunt who was away in Jamaica visiting family. She'd reserved her Key Largo home for the two of us. We ate breakfast in the gourmet white-tiled kitchen, dining on fresh fruit and yogurt from the generous supplies left for us in the fridge. Afterward, we carried our drinks out onto the front steps of the porch.

Snuggling on the swing, we sipped imported Jamaican coffee and admired the curved portico surrounded by columns, and the low-hanging palm trees that finished off this tropical scene.

Winston was never far away.

"Director of Chrysalis," she said. "Sounds so sexy."

"Glad you think so." I kissed the top of her head.

"When we get back to L.A., I'm going to arrange another charity event. Let's hold another one for Wells of Africa."

My favorite charity.

"I'm not ready to leave here," I whispered. "Not sure I ever will be."

"Me neither. I think I'd like to retire here. What do you think?"

"What? The two of us slowing down time and spending our days reading, walking, and making love? Sure you want that?"

She rested her head on my shoulder. "Nirvana."

I brought her hand to my lips and kissed her wrist.

"God, I love it here," she said. "No, that's not strictly true. It's you being here with me that changes everything."

"Someone's got it bad."

She slapped my arm playfully. "I'm not the only one."

"Why do you say that?"

"Yeah, I caught you watching that YouTube video of me."

"That was an advert, actually. I was forced to endure it so I could get to the video I was actually trying to see."

"Which was?"

"Some stock exchange documentary."

"Really?"

"Okay, I'll admit it was a clip from a movie coming out later this year. About a young woman becoming a millionaire's submissive. She's quite talented. If you like that sort of thing."

She thumped my arm again. "Someone's showing up on the red carpet with me."

"Winston," I called over. "Hear that? You're walking the red carpet."

He trotted over to us, his eyes darting from one to the other.

"I'm serious," she said. "I want you at the premiere."

"Then I'll be there."

"Let's make a normal life for us."

"With you, Andrea, life will never be normal." I threw her a grin.

"I want babies."

"Where did that come from?"

"Lots of them. Or, if you'd rather, we can adopt?"

"I'm more than capable of servicing your needs, missy."

She threw her head back in a laugh. "Say yes."

"Yes to what?"

"Us."

"I believe I did that first time you broke into my home like the wanton criminal you are."

"You knew then?"

"Suspected. How about you?"

"The moment you stepped into my office that first time. I couldn't breathe properly. You were so arrogant and sexy and didn't care who I was."

"I probably still owe you an apology for my behavior."

"Yes, you do. See that you make it up to me."

I quirked a smile. "I hear they organize diving excursions in town. Fancy a trip out on a boat tonight?"

She narrowed her gaze.

"I was thinking of a sunset cruise? No sharks allowed."

"Now that I'd enjoy."

"I'll book it then."

She leaned into me and the day began as I always hoped it would - with her in my arms.

I couldn't keep my hands off her. Whether we were merely snuggling on the porch swing or when we showered in the morning, our need to be together was overwhelming. The way she nurtured me, held me, listened so profoundly to all I had to say. And I enjoyed nothing more than lying on the couch, or on the bed, or even the floor, and listening to the sexy huskiness of her voice reassuring me all would be well with our world.

Her strength enriched mine.

Andrea was the woman I'd had no idea I needed.

She'd come into my world emboldened by her tenacious spirit and despite her initial fears she'd managed to move beyond them and save me from myself.

Every moment with her felt sacred.

We savored our vacation. Every happiness-drenched second of it.

The long days chasing after each other, slipping us into a future that delivered the kind of contentment that had eluded me until now.

I'd been a shipwreck caught in the storm. Through Andrea I'd found safe harbor.

Not allowing myself to love had been the darkest of all betrayals. A decision forced by my own hand, no less.

We deserved this mystery; this time was ours for us to grab and make our own.

All that we have in the end is our love.

And all my love was hers.

About the Author

Vanessa Fewings is the bestselling romance author of the highly acclaimed Enthrall Sessions.

Vanessa is also the author of The Stone Masters Vampire Series. Prior to publishing, Vanessa worked as a registered nurse and midwife. She holds a Masters Degree in Psychology. She has traveled extensively throughout the world and has lived in Germany, Hong Kong, and Cyprus.

Born and raised in England, Vanessa now proudly calls herself an American and resides in California with her husband.

Facebook: www.facebook.com/OfficialVMK

ENTHRALL SESSIONS:

1. Enthrall

2. Enthrall Her

3. Enthrall Him

4. Cameron's Control

5. Cameron's Contract

6. Richard's Reign

Made in United States
Troutdale, OR
08/07/2023

11858946R00108